VAMPIRE WARS

THE
BECOMING

Heather
Knox

EPIC Escape

An Imprint of EPIC Press
abdopublishing.com

The Becoming
Vampire Wars: Book #1

abdopublishing.com

Published by EPIC Press, a division of ABDO, PO Box 398166, Minneapolis, Minnesota 55439. Copyright © 2019 by Abdo Consulting Group, Inc. International copyrights reserved in all countries. No part of this book may be reproduced in any form without written permission from the publisher. Escape™ is a trademark and logo of EPIC Press.

Printed in the United States of America, North Mankato, Minnesota.

052018
092018

Cover design by Candice Keimig
Images for cover and interior art obtained from iStockphoto.com
Edited by Jennifer Skogen

Library of Congress Cataloging-in-Publication Data

Library of Congress Control Number: 2018932895

Publisher's Cataloging in Publication Data

Names: Knox, Heather, author.
Title: The becoming/ by Heather Knox
Description: Minneapolis, MN : EPIC Press, 2019 | Series: Vampire wars; #1
Summary: The death of Ezekiel "Zeke" Winter, an Elder Keeper, marks the uprising of the Praedari and the inclusion of humanity in their war. His descendant, Delilah, reveals his death as a murder and is given the opportunity to avenge him—and to potentially make a name for herself with the Keepers. With only her visions to guide her, Delilah must decide if the lives of four teenage captives and the promises of vengeance and glory are enough reason to risk her unlife.
Identifiers: ISBN 9781680769043 (lib. bdg.) | ISBN 9781680769326 (ebook)
Subjects: LCSH: Vampires--Fiction. | War--Fiction--Fiction. | Search and rescue operations--Fiction--Fiction. | Adventure stories--Fiction | Young adult fiction.
Classification: DDC [FIC]--dc23

For Sylvia Quinn

Now

WHEN THEY TELL ME ZEKE HAS DIED I GO WILD. I become gravity, heavy, pitching forward, falling. Two someones hold me just above the elbow, one on each side, maybe so I don't collapse into earthquake. Maybe so what happens next doesn't happen: I wrench free, shaking the someones off. Sob-screams rise from my stomach and tear from my throat as I see his torpid body. No one else sees. They see ash. I see Zeke's eyes widen slightly, exactly how it's written in cheap airport thrillers. He gasps, unaccustomed to needing breath, but whatever human is left inside him, vulnerable as a child, surfaces and tries not to die again.

You'd think the end would be more primal, the predator within fingering the shaft of wood before ripping it from his chest only just too late. But he dies gasping, uselessly, his human self finally won out against the monster—but they, the someones, see only ash and imagine the rest, if they care to. I'm sobbing, my cheek resting in a mirage of the pile of ash that is his chest which I feel and no one sees.

I'm left alone with my grief, wailing until the someones return. They pull me to my feet as though I may shatter. They're too late, I think, but I shuffle obediently to my room. A part of me no longer me murmurs *thank you*s. Still dressed, I lie in bed. The sky blues, ink diluted by the moment by water. Morning threatens from behind curtains I didn't close but that are somehow now closed. I sleep.

For twenty-seven nights I rise from my bed and

cross to the double doors that lead to the balcony. Pulling aside the thick curtains I catch a glimpse of someone in the glass, myself, logically, but also improbably not. Her hair falls in perfect dark curls, framing a puckered and grotesquely marred visage, like scar tissue, shiny and raw-seeming. Her eyes seem dull, a streetlight caped in fog. I leave the doors open behind me, slump to the cool tile at the balcony's edge and stare from between the wrought iron grates over the city.

For too many nights the city buzzes below, unaware of his passing. Unaware of him, of me, of *us*—the monsters that hunt them and feed from them but also protect them. Each morning, just before dawn, someone carries me, unresponsive, to the bed. Draws the curtains. Disappears. By his smell I recognize Caius, an Elder of the Everlasting probably being punished with this babysitting for some imperceptible offense or another in the Council chambers. Or maybe he cared for my Usher and takes care of me not out of obligation, but genuine fraternity. I soften at this, though improbable. Still, he feels more familiar to me than he should, as if we've shared a life I can't quite remember. Zeke often called me a romantic, a dying breed, he said, another of my many secrets. He told me this is probably why I survived the Becoming.

Before

"ZEKE, MAN, LISTEN—IF YOU WON'T, I WILL . . . "
Tomas says, eyeing the woman with the dark curls onstage as if he could devour her with his gaze alone. A woman walking behind him toys with the hair at the nape of his neck in passing. He slips a few twenties into the tip jar she carries, winks at her.

"Do you even know her name?" I joke.

Tomas shrugs, taking a swig of blood from a contraband flask he snuck in his jacket. We'd been coming to The Slaughterhouse together most nights for a few months now, since I began infiltrating Tomas's pack of Praedari.

The Slaughterhouse used to be a large commercial slaughterhouse, the uninspired name testament to the amount of work the owners put into restoring the building. The same tile floor, the drains now serving to keep spills and fallout from brawls tidy. Still, the pack claims this music club as part of their hunting grounds despite it being technically outside their territory. Praedari claims could be fluid like that as the strongest pack holding dominance until an even stronger one comes along.

"Name? Why would I need that? That guy's paid to announce it so I don't forget." He grins before turning his attention again to the stage.

I shake my head. I know her only as Delilah, probably her stage name. It is clear no one liked her—not the other singers, not the bartenders, not the bouncers. She makes no effort to be likeable, but when she sings she awakens something feral within you making it impossible not to love her or love hating her. Silky dark curls cascade down her back, somehow managing to never hide her face no matter how vigorously the music moves her. Her biceps and calves boast the lean muscle of a classically trained dancer; this grace underscored by the filth and sleaze of The Slaughterhouse. It is no wonder Tomas finds himself drawn to her. Unlike the other girls—who make every man feel like he's the only man she's ever sung for—Delilah sings only for herself.

Infiltration started as a reprieve from my often stifling duties as an Elder Keeper, and these visits to The Slaughterhouse started as a reprieve from my duties to Tomas's pack while I infiltrated, a way to take time away from them to focus on tactics and gain perspective. Then Tomas started tagging along. Rarely did others outside his pack have the chance to see through his bravado to get to know him, but his loyalty—to both his pack and the sect—could not be rivaled. I had no doubt he'd sacrifice his unlife for a packmate, which now included me.

As with Tomas, I began to notice things about Delilah that ran deeper than the surface. Something different in how the energy around her behaved. A sort of magnetism, as though many entities beyond my vision and awareness looked out for her. And, as unaware as she played at being, I noticed Delilah studying me. Perhaps she caught something predatory in my gaze. Something knowing—ancient, perhaps; intoxicating. Maybe this excites her.

Maybe I only wish for it to. Such is the spell she casts on you when she takes the stage. Still, last month she started ordering a drink—mineral water and lime; she never risks dulling her senses with alcohol in a place like this—and taking her time with it at the bar. Side by side we passed many nights, never speaking. Just strangers at the bar.

"Well, man, I'll give you as much time as I

can," Tomas starts, standing. Manners he lacks, but charm he has in spades, a Gift of his Blood. "Anyway, I've got some scouting to do," he says before heading out into the night.

Recruitment, how could I have forgotten? The pack's rumblings about recruitment have turned into a plan. We each need to provide a "recruit" for the Becoming, someone worthy of becoming one of the Everlasting, worthy of becoming one of the *Praedari*. Failure to do so would bring my loyalty into question and jeopardize the mission. I came here tonight to forget about that.

I rub my crinkled brow, staring at the stage but not seeing—instead, worrying about a way out of the upcoming rite. The music ending interrupts my thoughts. I see Delilah approach the edge of the stage, eyes wet and empty as if in a trance. She climbs down, seemingly unaware of the bills crumpled and stuffed into the tip jar on the edge of the stage behind her.

A man notices, though, and sees an opportunity

to reclaim his contribution. He rushes over, glancing around before greedily stuffing bills into his pockets. I'm on him in an instant, a feeling like boiling where my heart used to beat. I grab his arm and bend. I don't stop bending until I hear a satisfying snap, his screams rushing around me, white noise to that predatory thing within me, unnamed.

A bouncer approaches. He wears a gun tucked into the waistband of his jeans. I lock eyes with him. When he reaches where the man and I stand, he merely grabs the man by his uninjured arm and moves to drag him from the club.

"Wait," I interrupt. "He's got her money." I jerk my head towards the bar where Delilah sits.

The bouncer reaches roughly into the man's pockets and pulls out wads of bills, handing them to me before dragging him outside.

Delilah sits at the bar, her usual drink in front of her.

"Thanks for that, back there. Let me buy you a drink."

"No need." I keep my voice low, barely above a whisper.

"Shoot. Seems there's a bit of blood on your shirt," she says dipping a napkin into her glass and leaning forward to grab my collar. She moves like silk, dabbing at something I can't see. Her fingers rest against my neck a moment. I clear my throat.

She pulls her hands away, dropping the crumpled napkin on the bar. "Our options here are limited for how I can show my gratitude."

"I don't drink much."

"No, I suppose you don't." She smirks.

She finishes her mineral water, letting the glass meet the bar with a satisfying *thunk* before winking an invitation and heading backstage.

༄

I wait a few minutes, then follow. One meaningful

look and the bouncer waves me through the worn velvet rope. Backstage looms darker than I anticipated, and quieter.

"I bet you're thirsty." Delilah's voice, low and confident, comes from a room to the right. A light flickers above, dim, casting a flattering glow that illuminates her curves.

"What?"

"Don't play stupid."

I enter the dressing room to find her leaning against the wall next to a vanity covered in makeup, glitter, hairspray, Victoria's Secret bottles. Reflected in the too many mirrors, I see myself through the lens of the curse: a marred visage of puckered, decaying skin barely covering bone. For the first time in a century I find myself self-conscious, momentarily forgetting that should she catch my reflection, I'll appear just as I do in the flesh—young, strong, smooth. Such is the curse I'm intended to suffer alone. I narrow my eyes and turn away, back to her.

"Who are you?" I demand.

"Delilah—stage names are for those who're hiding from something."

I take a few steps toward her.

"I didn't mean your name and I'm guessing you know that. *What* are you?"

"Don't you mean *who* am I?"

"I asked what I wanted answered," I quip. "Twice now."

"Someone who isn't blind." She adjusts her hair in the mirror, then catches my eye in the reflection. I notice a copy of *Anna Karenina*, pages dog-eared, cover creased and worn and faded, half-buried by makeup compacts and dresses strewn carelessly between lounge acts. "You've been coming here for months and ordering drinks you don't *really* drink. You snapped a man's arm like a candy cane. You didn't bat an eye when I said you had blood on your collar. You don't breathe, and you have no pulse."

The napkin. No tinge of blood on it or my collar. She lingered to see if she could feel a pulse.

"The real question is," she continues, "how has no one else noticed?"

"What is it you think I am?" I ask.

"I've heard it's intense, more intense than anything." She turns to face me, dragging her hand slowly down her throat. "You can drink of me if you like."

The predator within me still lurks dangerously near the surface, riled up from before. I lunge for her, slamming her into the wall. She is right and this angers me, rouses that thing within that we Keepers fight so hard to swallow and dismiss. But we are alone. Why not? *No.* Her eyes grow wide for only a moment, her posture stiffening almost imperceptibly before relaxing once again.

"I've known others, *companions* to your kind. They became addicted."

"I could kill you with one hand," I snarl in her

ear. My hand moves to around her throat. I can feel her pulse. "You're so—"

"Delicate?"

"Helpless."

"Hardly," Delilah snorts. "I'm not some doe-eyed waif who's been chewed up and spat out by the city. But I wonder if you know that?"

I suspect no one knows anything about her unless she intends them to, myself included despite the hours that have slipped silently between us at the bar, despite the hours that have slipped silently between us as she takes the stage, despite feeling like she's as much a part of Tomas's pack passively and by circumstance as I've become intentionally. The mentality of a voyeur. She looks like she could be eighteen, nineteen—what am I doing? Even when I was made, centuries ago, I had more mileage on my mortal shell than she does now.

I relax my grip, take a step back. Was that—is she disappointed?

"Fine. I bet your friend will be back soon."

She takes a deep breath. Was she shaken? "He looked . . . hungry."

I watch the bruises bloom on her biceps.

"Don't worry," she says into the mirror. "They'll be gone soon enough."

My Beast clawing for a way out, shredding every ounce of willpower so I don't take her up on her offer. I can almost feel the delicate skin of her shoulder as my fingers dance along the ridge there, brushing her hair aside, her flesh giving way just as my fangs—no. Delilah knows too much for the comfort of the Keepers, courts disaster too much to go long unnoticed by the Praedari. If she moves in on one of my pack my cover will be blown— either when Tomas claims her for recruitment and I must violate his claim by killing her or when the pack questions my dedication to them because I showed the girl mercy and did not claim her as my own. The Praedari may tolerate a lot of dissent, but mercy and selfishness always meet a swift punishment. I know what I must do. Besides, a girl going missing in the city is hardly a headline and I need a recruit. There's no way she could survive the Becoming.

Less cleaning up to do.

3
Now

ON THE TWENTY-EIGHTH NIGHT I WAKE TO CAIUS sitting in the overstuffed chair in the corner of the room, one hand's fingers tapping impatiently on the arm, the other's mangled and knotted, dangling, limp. Likely an injury he incurred while alive, though the alternative, that he came up against something that powerful and survived, excites the predator within me.

Either the room or Caius smell musty, like damp earth tilled to the surface that hasn't properly dried in weeks. Spring after winter's thaw. I rise, as I have for weeks, and cross to the double doors that lead to the balcony. Pulling aside the thick curtains, I have a vision of Caius that dances over the glass where my reflection should be—younger, ugly, but not yet hideous. I blink longer than usual to clear the vision and leave the doors open behind me. The Gift of Sight often comes in short, murky flashes, sometimes a few times a night and then not again for months. Standing at the wrought iron grates, I feel him enter the doorway.

"The Council has summoned you," he states.

I. THE VISION OF THE FIRST ELDERS AS PERTAINS TO the Council of Keepers

The founding of the Council of Keepers, amended on this [day redacted] of [month redacted], [year redacted], ensures the continued vision of the First Ones.

i. That only from the shadows may we protect;

ii. That only by hiding our nature may we remain in the shadows;

iii. That only in controlling our Beast may we hide our nature;

iv. That only by strict observance of the Corpus Rituum Perpetuorum may we control our Beast.

As it is written, so shall it be enforced.

II. The Purpose of the Council of Keepers

The purpose of the Council of Keepers is to uphold the vision of the First Ones as set forth above. In doing so, it is the duty of the Council of Keepers to:

i. Maintain a strong presence in their territory so the enemy does not recruit from within;

ii. Meet dissent with swift-but-just means so protection of the mortal world is not compromised;

iii. Observe the Corpus Rituum Perpetuorum without err so the Council may be looked to as living the vision of the First Ones;

iv. Strive for consensus among the Council members in all major judgments so as to bolster the perception of cohesion.

As it is written, so shall it be observed.

III. The Structure of the Council of Keepers

The Council of Keepers shall be comprised of

the seven eldest Keepers in the territory. In the case of an Elder Keeper of significant age moving into a region, there shall be a formal contest between this Elder and the youngest serving on the Council. This contest shall include:

i. A test of wits;

ii. A test of endurance;

iii. A test of politesse;

iv. And a test of knowledge of the Corpus Rituum Perpetuorum.

The one defending their position on the Council may instead participate by champion, if another on the Council will take up the cause. This allows a Council within a territory to demonstrate the solidarity of their bond.

As it is written, so shall it be chosen.

IV. The Privilege of the Eldest of the Council of Keepers

It remains the privilege of the Eldest of the Council of Keepers to veto or hand-down a decree, so long as it upholds the vision of the First Ones and the purpose of the Council of Keepers.

As it is written, so shall it be.

5

Now

I TAKE A DEEP BREATH BEFORE SLUMPING TO THE tile. I trace the paths of grout. Probably this had been beautiful once, before the cracking and the mold. Caius returns early, bends down to offer me a mug of hot Earl Grey with his one good hand. For a moment I think Zeke has returned, that it's all part of one of our elaborate personal rites.

"Zeke said once that it soothes you."

I nod, staring into the mug. I inhale. Though we can't eat or drink, the ritual of making a cup of tea helps me burn nervous energy. Holding the hot mug between my corpse-cold hands and inhaling the steam helps me focus. Sometimes the steam scalds. I welcome the sharp pain. I never told Zeke that it reminds me not of my Becoming or my Binding, but of the time before, the life I can't remember living.

I try to ask *What do they want with me?* but I haven't spoken in so long the words become a sort of growling bark. Caius chuckles and tosses me something he pulls from his worn leather jacket: a blood donation bag. O-. The universal donor— though it doesn't matter for one of the Everlasting, some develop specific tastes as a mortal might with wine. I wonder where he got it but don't ask. I bite one of the valves and take a long sip, feigning, for a moment, delicacy. Then the hunger overtakes me and I drain the bag, licking my lips. Cold blood, as it is called, satisfies only the need for sustenance and does not sate the Beast's more savage impulses. My pupils dilate. My fangs emerge from my gums. I sniff the air. Their takeout containers, their garbage-filled alleyways, their sweat, gasoline. I think for a moment I can smell the stars. Zeke taught me how to rein in the urges that now bubble to the surface, a gamble Caius shouldn't have made unless he and Zeke were indeed close and spoke of my training. I'm breathing heavily, a habit from my mortal days now taken the form of the predator. I will my fangs to retract. I close my eyes, unclenching the empty PVC bag.

"You need to hunt," Caius scolds.

"Why have you returned?" I cough a couple times before I'm able to finish the question. My voice sounds like ocean echoing in a sea cave, though I'm sure only to me. Before Zeke's death, Caius hadn't visited the city for at least a decade, preferring quieter surroundings less steeped in the politics of the Everlasting.

Caius considers me before answering.

"A long time ago Zeke asked me to look after you if something should happen to him."

"Because I need to be looked after?" I challenge.

"Because you have not been granted autonomy,"

he explains. "It was not meant as an insult. Zeke knew you were more than capable of looking out for yourself. Besides, this was a long time ago."

"When?"

He sighs and sits in the overstuffed chair.

"I really didn't intend to have this conversation right now, but if you insist . . . Shortly after your Becoming." Shortly, of course, being relative when you are one of the undying.

"So you were close?"

"Like brothers."

I study him a moment before continuing, skeptical. "If you were like brothers—"

"—why didn't you see more of me?"

I nod.

"He loved me like a brother, but his love for you was even deeper. He was deep undercover in the Praedari pack but seemed to trust them more with you than he did the Keepers. Still, I served as liaison between him and the Council, until the raid that wiped out that pack. *Then* he informed the Council of your Becoming."

"Were you a part of the raid?"

"I was. I visited the two of you frequently during your Ritus Iungendi," he starts, using the old Latin name to refer to my Rite of Binding. "I'm not surprised you don't remember." I shake my head, the truth feeling familiar despite evading memory— why he felt so familiar, why my Beast wasn't rattled by the presence of another predator in my intimate space. He saw me at my most vulnerable, imprinting even through the haze of my Binding.

"But—"

"He trusted me with your secret, but only after trusting me with his life more than once. Still, he knew my Beast yearned to roam outside the confines of the city, that my being here too long would erode the predator in me."

"How long will you stay?"

"As long as I am needed. I'm here to look after you, as I promised."

I sob, his presence amplifying the absence that's consumed me since Zeke's death. Embarrassed by the sudden show of emotion, I turn my face away. Caius moves to the bed, putting his arm stiffly around me. He is silent for several moments, letting me sob and cry tears of blood onto the shoulder of his jacket.

"He died a good death, Delilah."

No matter which of the circulating rumors surrounding Zeke's death he speaks of, I know Caius to be right. There aren't many ways to kill one of the Everlasting, but often plenty of reasons one might be killed. Whether he infiltrated too deeply into the Praedari ranks or unearthed an ancient secret no one was meant to unearth, he died fighting. By Caius's statement, I know he knows this, too.

The tea has cooled considerably, my hands having sapped the warmth from both the water and the ceramic. I catch my reflection in its surface. This face that once was beautiful now bears more than the few years I've been one of the Everlasting, my countenance, knit of the tortuous Ritus Iungendi and my Becoming, concealing my age.

"Don't . . . " he says quietly, cupping my chin to gently tilt my face up to meet his gaze. "You are more than what you've been through. You are more than this."

Some of the Everlasting took to the shadows centuries ago, calling themselves the Keepers and concealing their nature to protect humanity as much as themselves. Why Zeke never mentioned our relationship to Caius I'll never know—to protect me? Caius? Himself? But because he didn't, I assumed Caius, like most, did not know why Zeke chose me for the Becoming. Did not know that Zeke miscalculated my strength, or something like it—that he never intended me to survive.

6

Before

I BREATHE IN DIRT. DARKNESS AND DIRT. IF I AM TO live I have to find up. I claw and claw. Nowhere to move dirt to because I am surrounded by it. I kick and kick and claw and kick. Except dirt holds me in place. I writhe and claw. I think I scream but dirt eats the sound. I eat dirt. I breathe dirt. I become dirt. I am dirt.

Somehow I move in a direction I only pretend to know as up. I think I see a flash of something outpace me. Then dirt. I realize I am seeing, so I keep clawing in the direction I think is up. My fingers graze something soft and cold, a different soft and cold than dirt. Flesh. Another buried like me but unmoving. I scream but the dirt absorbs the sound. I tear at the soil, the musk of earth and decay in my nostrils.

My hand reaches through and past. Cool air. Space. Open. I claw and claw and emerge gasping, coughing, choking except I'm not and somehow I'm alive and not. I do not feel my heart racing though I hear the thump-thump of it. I do not feel fear. Screams, my own, another's. I cannot tell which screams echo in my head and which resonate in the night. I cannot tell which are my own. I lunge towards something warm and slow. That is the heart I hear.

Hot liquid rushes past my lips, caressing my throat. Some drips down my chin onto my chest. I hear droplets hit the earth, the fresh-tilled soil, like tears on a pillow. Shapes move around me. I feel them but do not see. Only darkness and the liquid which now burns my throat as it fills me. I keep sucking but this vessel yields nothing. I turn.

I lunge but this something is the temperature of night, and fast. I am aware that someone speaks but I do not understand. A part of me, not me—but, at the same time, all of me—growls and lunges again. I hit the ground hard. No heartbeat but I smell blood. My own, another's—and his. Everything echoes. I breathe deeply and attempt to focus, pushing down this new part of me that growls and lunges and isn't me. Swallowing instinct, impulse, I sputter, coughing up dirt. I am lying on the ground on my side. How did I get here? Particles of dirt and droplets of blood spatter the dew-soaked grass.

Someone speaks. I groan and roll onto my back. Echoing turns to spinning. Darkness. Stars. Night. A man's voice. A man kneels next to me. How long has he been there?

"That's it. Focus," the man says. He chuckles, shaking his head. "I didn't think I'd see you again, Delilah. You're full of surprises."

I blink.

"Can you hear me?"

I nod.

"Delilah?"

I stare at him. The name rings in my ears as familiar, but only distantly so.

Delilah. Delilah. Delilah.

I furrow my brow. Why does he keep saying that name?

"Your name is Delilah," he says, answering a question I did or didn't ask. "You're one of the Everlasting now."

He extends his hand to me to help me sit up. I hesitate, then reach out. When my skin meets his, the world spins again. My eyes widen. He shifts and I feel his arms wrap around me. At first I feel that I'm trembling, becoming earthquake. Then I see myself trembling in this stranger's embrace. I've stepped outside myself.

৶৶

Then the world shifts again. I turn. Behind me I

am trembling in this stranger's arms, but in front of me four teenagers lie sleeping, tubes like IVs in each of their arms. I cannot see to what they are connected—beyond them I see only the dirt I've climbed out from and a mangled shape slumped, surrounded by a dark pool.

I walk towards the wet and smell a familiar metallic tang. In the mirror-like surface stars appear as tiny flecks of light around my face. They flit like fireflies. My hair matted with dirt and my face caked with dark; nausea washes over me. The reflection swirls and changes to that of a beautiful woman, pale, sleeping like the four teenagers but with a thick tube down her throat rather than in her arms like IVs. She feels familiar. Bound at the wrists and ankles. I want to touch her. I think of Snow White. Then of the poison apple.

Time passes.

Her eyes open.

I can feel her hunger.

Where I was embraced I'm now restrained. I snarl. The man restraining me shows no strain, as if I'm made of paper, a weightless thing. Through my anger—anger? hunger? fear? —I think that a strong enough night breeze might take me far away from here forever. An emptiness sets in, yawns on endlessly in only an instant. I snap my jaws at the stranger.

I can hear his voice, but I can't make out the words. Still, something inside of me calms and I am left babbling about Snow White and the Huntsman, that old fairytale, how he took my liver and lungs. When I breathe in I feel hollow. The smell of soil and blood and cologne, earthy and decaying and metallic and spicy and woody, all emanate from this stranger. From me. From this place. My focus shifts to what I can see: a cemetery, freshly clawed-up soil in a few places, just a few feet from one another. The discolored fingers of a rogue hand poke up from the dirt like pale crocuses, another like me but who did not emerge from the mass grave as I did. A few feet away another mangled shape slumps against a low mound of dirt, into which a shovel has been plunged so it stands erect, a sort of flag. I get the sense I've conquered something but I'm not sure what. A dark pool has gathered around the slumped form. My eyes linger here.

"There," I say in a voice much more my own. "That's where I saw her."

"Who?" the man asks.

"Snow Wh—a woman. She had a tube down her throat and someone bound her to a bed."

"What else?"

I shake my head. He loosens his grip on me, shifting to kneel beside me, no longer looming, a less imposing posture.

"Delilah, try to remember."

Tears sting my eyes.

"I—I can't!"

"Okay! Okay," his tone softens as he cradles me. "It's okay. I'm here. You're here. You had a vision. It's not here. It can't harm you."

Somehow I am soothed, like a child who's skinned their knee: it still hurts, or the memory of it hurts, until the Band-Aid. The rational part of my brain screams—*He's a stranger! You just climbed out of a grave! He buried you alive! You killed someone! What is going on?*—but something in his voice quells the noise. I look up at him with questioning eyes and am lucky that I needn't form the words.

"I'm Zeke, your Usher—the one that made you a vampire, one of the Everlasting. Tonight was your Becoming. My Usher had visions like you." Before I can say anything, he continues. "We should go. The others will return soon. The rite is not over."

He helps me stand.

"Will you let me keep you safe?" he asks, eyes holding my own in their gaze.

"Do I have a choice?"

7

Now

THE BACK HALF OF THE ART ROOM SERVES AS THE workroom for the school newspaper. Kiley sighs as she enters the empty room, accustomed to only meeting Monday, Wednesday, Friday but as this week's editor, she wants to get a head start on copyediting. She's always been a bit of a perfectionist. Not, like, unhealthily so, but enough to irritate other people and always end up the leader in groupwork. That's why she's drawn to paranormal investigation—there's nothing perfect or foolproof when you're looking for ghosts and sometimes it's nice to take a break from yourself.

Settling in to begin her edits, she rakes her hands through the thick mess of hair atop her head, wrestling it into something like a ponytail with wisps around her face refusing to be tamed. The corner of a bright pink sticky note sticking out from the stack catches her attention. The note is attached to an article she wrote on the story behind the cursed gymnasium, wherein she debunks the theory as a lame attempt at justifying the fact that their basketball team hasn't won, or come close to winning, a single home game since 1990—and rarely an away one. They no longer have a cheerleading squad for basketball season because the cost of new uniforms and trips to away games just to cheer for a losing team couldn't be rationalized as a proper use of alumnae-donated funding. She's been waiting until her week as editor, knowing that's the only way she'd get away with such an exposé. Plus her article doesn't mention God once which is pretty much a sin in a private Catholic school like theirs.

The thing is, though, she never turned in this

story. Why would she as the editor this issue? Layout is Friday. Yet, here it is, on Tuesday, attached to her article, in black Sharpie scrawled across neon pink sticky note: "Want proof?"

There's another pink sticky note underneath this one: "113 Maple Drive. Midnight." The old church with the schoolhouse across the street, another supposedly haunted site just outside town. People say that if you go there at midnight on the night of the full moon and lie across the street—lined up so that you serve as a sort of bridge between the church door and the door of the schoolhouse—a parade of ghost-children holding hands will walk across you from the schoolhouse into the church to pray. The children, victims of a field-trip bus accident or ritualistic murderers themselves à la *Children of the Corn*, depending who tells the story, will bring you with them, the parade pausing so the last can hold their hand out to you, beckoning you to join them in death. As usually goes with ghosts, you really don't have a choice.

Kiley arrives early, having no idea what this proof might relate to—the curse? the budget cuts? the ghost-children?—but no journalist or paranormal investigator would write off a potential source without at least listening to them first, so she waits.

Both buildings long since abandoned and boarded up, only the church shows any sign of visitors. A shutter creaks, having been pried up. A couple beer cans sit on the steps. The schoolhouse, though, remains untouched, pristine save for a little disrepair brought on by time: paint cracked and peeling, steps sagging and warped from years of sun-rain-snow-rain-sun. Apparently, despite the site's close proximity to a parochial school, kids sneaking out would rather anger God than some ghost-children.

Not one to waste a good sneaking-out herself, she has grabbed the vintage Nikon FE film camera she got for Christmas and heads up to the church. She snaps pictures, multiples from the same angle, aiming for clarity rather than being artistic. Even if someone on staff is just playing a prank, maybe something interesting will turn up on film to justify her sneaking out at this hour. Especially since there's a solid chance she'll get caught *and* grounded.

She turns her head when she hears a sound not unlike the creaking shutter but from the rear of the church. Camera ready, she slinks around the side of the building. At the corner, she shoves the camera in front of her, angled towards the sound and snaps a picture. Then she follows, stepping around the corner.

Nothing.

She breathes out, relieved, and laughs a little at herself, shaking her head. Glancing at her watch, she notes the time and heads back towards the road. Still no sign of another soul, alive or other-wise, and no other vehicle but hers pulled over on the dirt shoulder. Given the time and distance from town, she doesn't expect someone to happen upon her. She crosses to the schoolhouse to take more pictures.

Footsteps, not on grass as she is, but sidewalk. She turns to greet the sound, but no one's there. Unlike most visitors to the site, she doesn't give wider berth to the schoolhouse, using the same techniques she used for photographing the church. She finds a window where the boards have been nailed leaving a gap not thicker than an iPhone, through which she snaps dozens of pictures, zooming in and back out, adjusting shutter speed and aperture to maximize her chances of catching something on film. Her breath catches in her throat as she feels something move very quickly behind and past her. Spinning around, she scans the area behind her. Not so much as a blade of grass seems disturbed.

Out of film and still a few minutes to kill. Just two minutes until midnight, according to her phone. She wonders if ghosts are as precise? Almost all ghost stories involve the stroke of midnight. She resolves to not make this a wasted trip—if the note in the art room was a prank, at least she could salvage her night and make sneaking out worth it.

She crosses the road, pausing in the center. She glances to the church, then the schoolhouse. The clock turns to 11:59 p.m. *Now or never*, she thinks, laying down in the road, lining herself up with both doors as the story goes. She smooths her skirt nervously, resists wiggling one saddle-shoed foot. She closes her eyes, taking a deep breath.

The hairs on the back of her neck rise.

"Boo," says a female voice rather flatly, startling Kiley's eyes open.

She's looking up at a girl about her age, gray skate-style shoes nearly grazing her temples, though Kiley didn't hear her approach. She wears a worn black T-shirt, cropped—or ripped—that reads "feminist killjoy," the screenprint having seen better days. A thick lock of Kiley's hair has escaped its ponytail and now lays partially trapped underneath the girl's left foot. The girl's arms are crossed as she looks down at Kiley.

"Why're you laying like that?"

"Who're you?"

"The caretaker. Why're you laying like that?" she repeats.

Kiley raises an eyebrow. She shakes her head to indicate no, but the motion is cut short as the shoe pulls painfully on her hair.

"You're not the caretaker," Kiley accuses.

"Nah, you're right. I'm not," the girl admits. Her lips curl into a smile, sharp cuspids showing.

"I'm a vampire."

Before

"Y ou'll need to disappear, Delilah. Will anyone come looking for you?"

I shrug and then shake my head.

"Maybe. I don't know."

I fiddle with a loose thread in the upholstery of a chair that looks too expensive for this simple apartment. I've showered and am wearing an undershirt of Zeke's and a pair of loose-fitting sweatpants. I smell my bloodied rags in a black trash bag by the door.

"We'll deal with that if they come looking, then. From now on, you're dead. There's nothing left in their world for you now." He draws thick curtains closed. "You're a vampire now. Sunlight will kill you—you won't bloody *glitter*, you'll burst into flames and turn into ash. Holy water will burn you in the same way, but if you somehow fall into a vat of holy water you're probably leaving behind bigger problems for us to clean up. Anything blessed that pierces your flesh will turn you to ash. That other garbage—garlic, running water, crosses, needing an invitation to cross a threshold—that's Hollywood. You're not immortal, but if you play your cards right you're pretty close."

"I drink blood?" I finally ask, voice steady, avoiding eye contact.

He nods. "We drink blood. You won't be able to keep anything other than blood down and it's a waste of energy to try. Delilah, you need to understand something—" He crosses to kneel in front of me. He lifts my chin to meet his gaze. "We're Keepers. We don't kill. Not intentionally and certainly not often."

"But tonight—"

"Tonight we were Praedari. I've been infiltrating this pack for a while now. The Praedari, they embrace the Beast and believe it their right to hunt and kill indiscriminately. They are hunters, whether solitary or in a pack, and aren't to be trusted. As Keepers, we seek to control our Beast and protect the mortal world from the Praedari, and worse."

"The Beast?" Even as the question tumbles from my lips I know the answer. The Beast. Maybe I don't have a soul anymore and this thing fills that void. Maybe where my heart once beat it now lurks. Geography of my anatomy and this transformation aside, I understand.

Zeke has answered and moves on as I become aware again that he speaks. "There was a time when we weren't thought of as monsters because we simply weren't thought of. We remained in the shadows, hunting but protecting. But times are changing, Delilah. Now we are on the verge of war—the Keepers with the Praedari, the Everlasting with humanity."

He continues. "I am your Usher, the one who guided you through your Becoming. Except that no Keeper has gone through what you have because that was one of the Praedari's savage traditions. Normally it's far less traumatic—pleasant, even."

I find it hard to believe that being dead and then suddenly being not dead could be, as he describes, pleasant. Even so, a faint sensation bubbles forth at two points in my neck, warm and electric, and I bite my lip at the quasi-thought of something I can't quite remember. I feel a subtle flush creep into my cheeks so I glance around the room as he speaks to avoid him seeing. I can read every title on the bookshelf, even in this dim light, and distract myself by committing them to memory. The black trash bag by the door should conceal the smell of my bloody clothes, I realize, but it's as if I'm bathing in the metallic odor. Outside, sounds of life carrying on: wet tires humming on the street, transformers buzzing, a siren too many miles off, stilettos clicking on sidewalk.

I stand and cross to a window, tugging up, the window nearly tearing out of the frame as it crashes to the top. I need air. I try to breathe deeply but am assaulted by the stench of days-old fried egg rolls baked onto the metal bottom of a dumpster and floor shifting underneath me. My fingertips graze the windowsill as I fail to catch myself.

"Oh!" Zeke is behind me in a flash, steadying me.

"Too much . . . " I manage to explain as he lifts me back to the chair.

"You're overwhelmed—your senses are in overdrive. That will calm down some, but all Everlasting gain heightened sensory awareness. You'll adjust to it. You'll find that you're also stronger, faster, and more graceful than most mortals. You're a predator now. These Gifts belong to all Everlasting."

He brushes a stray curl of hair from my eyes, his

touch lingering just a moment too long before he notices I notice. He recoils his hand as if I'm fire.

"Other Gifts are passed through the Blood, are distinctive of our lineage. That's likely where your visions come from. Sometimes these Gifts skip generations, but eventually those that have roots in your Blood will manifest and bloom given some time and attention. Some of these come at a price— like how we can sense the ebb and flow of the Beast in others, but we feel more deeply than other Everlasting. Where others may get angry, our Beast rages. Where others develop a sense of loyalty or duty, ours swells to devotion, even obsession." He hesitates a moment. "We can bury it, but at great personal cost. Too often those of our lineage burn out rather than seek release," he warns, his gaze meeting mine only after skimming my legs upward, coming to rest at my lips before he catches himself. I notice, but do not say anything.

He continues with a quick bark of throat-clearing. "And all of this could be exploited by others, so it is often best not to flaunt what you're capable of around other Everlasting. Of course, others disagree, using this tactic to intimidate. Watch them, memorize their strengths, exploit them when you need to—but trust no one."

"Now what?" I ask after a brief pause.

"'Now what?' That's your response to all of this?"

I notice for the first time that he is handsome, rugged and dangerous, but his eyes softer than I would have guessed, skin smooth with just a bit of stubble. He's young, though older than me, maybe in his mid-to-late twenties. Smells like spice and wood and it's taken me this long to realize he doesn't wear cologne. The scent of something within him. His pupils dilate slightly. My Beast stirs but this time I do not thirst.

I lean forward and put my hand on the back of his neck. My lips nearly brush his. My heart doesn't beat but I feel the phantom twinge of it racing in my rib cage, like an amputee might feel an arm no longer there.

"I don't remember anything before your fangs in my neck. Now is everything. Now is all I have," I whisper before kissing him. He returns the kiss, pulling me to the edge of the chair. He stands. I gasp at his strength, more than human, and I wrestle with those words even as I run my hands through his hair.

"You feel this way because of the blood, because you're mine," he murmurs in my ear. The two points on my neck where once his fangs sank into my flesh alight with a desire that emanates outward, enveloping me.

"Why don't you let me decide how I feel."

After

LOOKING BACK, I KNOW THAT I HAD NO CHOICE IN whether, after my Becoming, I went with him. No choice in whether I wished him to keep me safe. No choice in trusting. I had no recollection of who I was before, what life I may have led. Covered in grave and blood, and Zeke—Ezekiel Winter, an Elder of the Keepers, my Usher whose blood awakened the Beast in me—in that moment he became at once my past, present, and future. The Everlasting liken it more to obsession than to true love. Even now I'm not sure.

Whatever might have been there—grown from

genuine affection or a by-product of the Blood—the Rite of Binding amplified. Each Usher has their own version, passed through their bloodline, but the basis of the ritual among the Keepers remains the same: to build a sense of trust in one's Usher and, by extension, the Elders; to pledge service to the sect and, by extension, the Elders; and to come face-to-face with one's Beast without succumbing to it. In essence, to fully embrace this new existence and weed out those too weak to survive, those that might become liabilities to the sect.

Some rites are cruel, excruciating rights of torture that last years, designed to break the new Everlasting of all ties to her past and condition her to need her Usher. Such codependent, abusive relationships rarely end well for the Usher and superstition surrounding this has led some to refuse to Usher at all. Other Binding rites echo the humane, forging something like loving bonds over time as with a caretaker, though a certain degree of codependency still plagues these Everlasting. More than one story has been told of a young Everlasting, still under the care of his Usher, who loved him so much he only wished to show him the beauty of a sunrise one final time—and with disastrous, ashy results for both. Still others rely heavily on the mysticism and the pageantry of elaborate ceremonies to bring Usher and Childe together—whether the magic of these rites is indeed *magic* or the bonding that takes place when sharing in something forbidden and secret, I'm not sure.

None of these—and all of these—characterize the Binding of my Bloodline.

Before

You've done well, Delilah, he said seconds or hours ago, before I heard a heavy door seal shut and his footsteps grow fainter as they retreated behind it.

I'm bound at the wrists by rough ropes reinforced by steel cable, a fact I discovered when I tried to chew through them in a moment of weakness. Wrists raw, steel cable now threatens to bite into nearly-exposed ligaments, my weight allowing no reprieve from the pain by virtue of gravity. I lean my head back, looking up at the rafters from which I'm hung. Black spots dance at the edge of my field of vision. At once I am both weightless and infinitely heavy, nothing and everything in this moment. Molecules of time writhe around me, trickle from my wrists down my arms. If I stretch, I can touch the floor with tiptoes, though it does nothing to alleviate my suffering.

I hear Zeke's footsteps approaching so I let my head loll to the side and forward, eyes closed. Maybe if he thinks I am unconscious I can steal an hour or two of silence. My body begs for silence. I wince when the first slash of the ceremonial dagger tears into the taut fleshy shallows of my abdomen. I cry out with the second, eyes widening, pupils dilating. That familiar warmth boils to inferno underneath the surface as my Beast reawakens. I growl. Another strike. I roar, my body lurching forward within the confinement of my bindings towards the one who strikes me: Zeke.

He's taken leave of the pack, citing his absence under the cloak of something far more perverse than this in the name of bonding. They do not question it—unlike the Keepers, the Praedari respect the right of the Usher to train his Childe in his own traditions for a short time before formally introducing them as one of the Everlasting or, in this case, initiating me formally into the pack. The allowance, of course, more a matter of convenience than sentimentality: part of this time is spent testing the young Everlasting, making sure they prove worthy of the pack's brotherhood. Survival alone proves heartiness, but proving dedication takes a more delicate touch. I repress a shudder as I think of what the others have been through at the hand of their Usher—and what others will go through at their hand. To belong to the pack, I must first belong to Zeke—so they leave us alone.

He holds in his hand a ceremonial dagger, the blade almost woven of metals whose colors I don't recognize and could not name, barbs spotting one edge, all of it attached to a polished wooden handle. Jagged fragments of something catch in the dim lighting, pinpoints of reflection dancing on the floor, my flesh, the wall like stars. I blink, wondering if I am imagining the light.

"More than just a blade—forged in a technique passed down from my Usher. I chose these metals especially for you, Delilah. Torture has long been used to extract information from the condemned, though most die in the process. As Everlasting, we stand condemned to an eternity of inner struggle—a struggle most Everlasting finally lose. But not us, not those of *our* Blood. Let the Keepers deny their struggle and cling to their own antiquated customs. Let the Praedari stay slave to barbaric rituals whose purpose has long since been lost to time. Thus we endure these rites in secret, away from the prying eyes of the Keepers and the Praedari who would not understand the lessons to be sought within them. Right now there's only you and this—"

I cry out as the blade slashes my skin, the barbs feeling as though they tear out shards of my flesh as they drag across. Tears roll down my cheeks as I'm struck again and again.

"Our bloodline uses suffering to transcend ourselves, to free ourselves of the fragile shell of our own mortality. Others cling to what they were. They cannot be trusted, for they are weak. Only through suffering can we come face-to-face with our Beast and only in this way can we control it."

Zeke circles me as he speaks. "If we can't do that, it is best we die our Final Death so we may spare our bloodline the shame of failure. Do you understand?"

I nod, the room wavering as though on the brink of a vision. I feel him step in close behind me, the hand not holding the blade moving firmly to my arm, as though to steady me. The dizziness responds to his touch, ebbing. He kisses my cheek and wipes away a tear.

"I'm here. You're here. Nothing can harm you. You are more than this."

He coaches me to take deep breaths, each

inhale expanding my lungs and stretching my torn flesh. Though as one of the Everlasting I need not breathe, the act serves as a sort of security blanket, soothing my nerves. I feel my Beast quieting, slinking in submission to a far corner of my soul, waiting for a moment of weakness from which to pounce.

"There. You're doing great. Breathe, if that helps, if it is still instinct. You will overcome that echo of your former self, but rely on it now if it soothes you. Shall we continue?"

I lock eyes with Zeke, my voice such that it could command the stars to bow to earth.

"Yes. I'm ready."

11

After

*N*OW WHAT? ZEKE WAS RIGHT THAT FIRST NIGHT.
Such a subdued response was bound to erupt
into something violent, something that would
change everything forever, though neither of us
could be sure when. The funny thing about time
when you're immortal is that it at once becomes
both irrelevant and everything.

The next few weeks blurred into months into
years before I was able to embrace what I'd become.
I tried to kill him more than once. I tried to kill
myself more than once. And I killed more times
than I can remember, each corpse bringing me

closer to the predator within, each corpse a mess for Zeke to clean up.

But I won't bore you with that.

Before

"**E**ZEKIEL, BROTHER," CAIUS CLASPS MY HAND firmly in his and pulls me in for a hug, clapping me roughly on the back with a few hollow thuds. A greeting between warriors, between brothers.

"I'm glad you could make it on such short notice. Did you have difficulty entering the territory?"

"What good's a lone wolf like me if I can't slip in and out undetected?" His teeth gleam, the smile of a predator, confident.

"Good. The packs that patrol the border have

been on high alert since the Howling is nearly upon us. It's almost as if they just got word of a Keeper infiltrating somewhere within the territory . . . " I smirk.

Caius laughs, though his nose crinkles in concern. "I wonder where they heard that?"

I shrug innocently, then join him in laughter.

"Tell me you have a decoy, at least?" he asks once his laughter subsides, but I wave it off. "What about her?" Caius asks, indicating Delilah suspended limp from the rafters, head lolled to the side, eyes closed. Blood stains the grout between tiles in the floor. Wet droplets still decorate the tile, splatters forming constellations of bright red against the dingy.

"She's fine, resting. You may speak freely in front of her," I say. There's nothing he could say that I need to shield her from. As we approach the end of her Binding, I know I can trust her implicitly—it is not as some Ushers would have their Childe, a quivering shadow of who they once were, afraid of angering their Usher, good for nothing more than errands or agreeing with their every whim. No, she will survive this, as I did, as my Usher did, and hers and further back than I can trace our lineage, and each of us stronger for it.

"This is her Binding Ritus?" Though Caius attempts to hide judgment, it's impossible not to notice the quirked eyebrow and amusement in his voice. Very few could I trust in this space, the reek of blood enough to awaken the predator within even the most seasoned Everlasting, the most precious thing in the world to me strung up like a fresh kill, on display, vulnerable. A little judgment, a little snark, is nothing between brothers.

"It is. Just as my Usher led me through the pain to become one of the Everlasting, so too I've led Delilah."

"Isn't that what the Becoming is for? Pleasant, perhaps, but not easy. Not all survive even our rites."

He's right. For most of us—for the Keepers, at

least, who still follow the old ways untainted by the savage customs championed by the Praedari. It hurts just a moment as your Usher's fangs pierce your flesh, but that pain quickly gives way to sensations no mortal could fathom, a flood of endorphins and oxytocin that no mortal could *survive* were they not, in that instant, becoming something more than themselves. The intimacy of drinking someone's life charges the Usher with something like the electricity of a first kiss, that breathlessness, something akin to what their Childe feels in that moment, albeit a sick approximation of that same pure pleasure that courses through their mortal veins in those final seconds. Most, then, Become, and do so quickly: their mortality slipping seamlessly into the night, replaced without pause by the hot blood of a fresh kill put gently to their lips by their Usher who guides them in sating their thirst.

Those selected by Keepers for the Becoming are courted, groomed, wooed, not ambushed and buried and left to die for the sake of some barbaric custom. The Keepers boast their fair share of regretful moments in the Corpus Rituum Perpetuorum, but I have yet to participate in a Praedari rite that did not force me to reconsider the worth of the mission as weighed against the loss of a part of myself. Not a moment passes that I don't regret what I did to her to Usher her. I spoke to Caius of it once and haven't spoken of it to anyone since.

"The Becoming physically transforms us. The Binding is what Ushers the soul, what shapes us into the Everlasting we will become. At any point she can ask to stop. Nothing happens without her consent. Still, it is not uncommon for one to lose themselves to the Beast within during this rite. A regrettable possibility, but one all the same."

"This," he indicates again Delilah, "makes sense for Ismae the Bloody. You, though?"

I shrug. "What was yours like?"

"Mine was sort of . . . an anti-Binding ritual. I spent the time alone, far away from other

Everlasting, far away from everything, really. The Becoming tested my physical endurance; the Binding, my ability to both sate and keep at bay the predator within. We spend too much time ignoring the balance we need to survive, afraid that by communing with the Beast-half of our soul we risk becoming the enemy, or worse. But our Beast-self is a part of us, nonetheless. Starving it ensures it rises up and seizes control, if not now, then later."

I consider this, my attention on my Childe—hurt, but not harmed. He's right, of course. In a sense, all Everlasting strive to teach balance in their own way, if not out of obligation of caretaking, then out of self-preservation. After all, before an Usher petitions the Council for Autonomy for their Childe, who does that Childe spend the majority of their time with? Which other predator within might they feel threatened by?

Like most things in the world, balance isn't all or nothing, but exists on a spectrum. By attempting to maintain existence somewhere between the extremes of hunter and hunted, we ensure that we don't succumb to the predator within and lose ourselves entirely. Caius exists somewhere between the center and the Beast, choosing to seek this balance by spending time with other hunters, with the wild, allowing his predator within to thrive but not take control.

When Ismae Ushered entire armies to fight for her empire, where did she fall on the spectrum? What about after, when her empire was secured, when she slaughtered all those she'd made? And then when she rose up against the Keepers after they offered her a title, prestige? Where did she fall then? What about me? And Delilah, where will she fall?

"Brother? You've gone elsewhere." Caius's voice interrupts my thoughts.

"Sorry—as grueling as it's been for her, so has it been for me." I offer a weak smile.

"Are you still cleaning up her messes?"

"She's learning to control herself. We all had to learn."

"I'm surprised you would willingly take this much time from your pursuit of the Valkyries. How long would you have tolerated her mistakes from another?" he asks. He narrows his eyes, studying me. "You care for the girl."

"Of course, I am her Usher."

"No. You *care* for her, in the way most our age can no longer. You love her." Though he spends much of his time removed from the company of other Everlasting, his insight remains as sharp as that of those who cannot go but a few nights without contact.

"And if I do?"

"It's a risk. Caring for something means it can be taken away," Caius warns.

"We're talking about a person, not someone's lucky T-shirt," I quip.

He waves my comment away. "All the same at

our age, isn't it? Have you considered the trauma she endured during her Becoming?"

"Does it matter?" I shrug.

"What if she can't heal, Ezekiel? The Praedari use that method of indoctrination because it *works*, because it breaks their recruits. And then to put her through *this* for the sake of preserving a Bloodline tradition?" He indicates the room with a sweeping gesture of his right arm as he leans forward, the fingers there mangled and useless most nights, save for when he chooses to expend the energy to heal the wound he sustained so long ago, which I've never known him to bother with.

"Who am I to judge whether she's healed?" I offer.

"You keep answering in questions, Zeke. Maybe what you should be asking is whether she feels the same for you. And why."

Transcribed from a Praedari rally at [location unknown] on June 13, 2001.

SPEAKER: Brothers and sisters in noctis!

We come together on this sacred night to honor those fallen brothers and sisters who held their ground against [*audio unclear*] forces. They embody what we as Praedari stand for and strive for. Without them our Blood is diminished.

CROWD: In their names we replenish the Blood!

SPEAKER: Tonight let us mourn not our loss, but celebrate the Becoming of our newest brothers and sisters—for they are our future. They do not yet know for what they are chosen, nor what trials they may face.

CROWD: But Praedari never face these trials alone!

SPEAKER: And this is our strength! Some of our brothers and sisters prefer the solitary hunt. We do not shun them, but instead welcome them each full moon with open arms and open veins.

CROWD: For no blood is lost between brothers and sisters!

SPEAKER: Some of our brothers and sisters prefer to hunt as a pack and each full moon we embrace them, share with them the honor of the Sacred Hunt.

CROWD: For no blood is lost between brothers and sisters!

SPEAKER: Let us now be reminded of the Code of the Praedari, as our Ushers spoke it to us and as our Ushers' Ushers spoke it to them—and so on, since the first Praedari became Praedari, refusing to hide in the shadows, refusing to bow to the Keepers' will, refusing to let the weak keep ruling the strong.

CROWD: We shall not hide, for we are the shadows! We shall not deny our Beast, for our Beast is who we've become! We shall not bear our throat to our enemy, for submission runs not in our blood! We shall not be afraid of the kill, for we've each died and only in that death become Praedari!

SPEAKER: We do not fight for some stodgy Elder that handed down a decree centuries ago. Let them keep their castles. Let them keep their councils and their chivalry and their cattle. We fight for now. We fight for us, for our brothers and our sisters. We fight to preserve the natural order: we are the predators, humanity the prey.

CROWD: It is not the burden of the lion to protect the gazelle!

[*Cheering.*]

[*End transmission.*]

14

Now

"HERE KITTY KITTY . . . " SAYS THE SNEERING Man with the pockmarked face. Ugly, even in the streetlight his teeth glow yellow, crooked like a fence that's been mended too many times. Hunter thinks of his cousins overseas who lost the battle between good genes and too many rough rugby matches.

"I can't believe I'm packed with you," says a girl who rolls her eyes and snaps her gum. Maybe fourteen, the youngest of the bunch but easily the fastest. She reminds Hunter of Selina Kyle, Catwoman before she was Catwoman, still with superhuman grace but clad in Dickensian-orphan sort of clothing rather than a latex catsuit, a black cropped T-shirt boasting in screenprint something in what might be French, a band name or a suggestion. The T-shirt: adorned with an obscene number of holes—some having worn with time and some perhaps intentional. She'd outgrow cute in another couple years, if she could find a shower. In another place, at another time Hunter might even ask her out if they weren't trying to . . . what? Kill him? Kidnap him? Mug him?

"If we're playing cat-and-mouse, isn't he the mouse?" another man speaks. He has an accent Hunter can't place, somewhere that isn't here.

"Huh?" Sneering Man asks.

"In your metaphor," the Foreigner replies before shaking his head and sighing.

"Can we just find the kid already?" the Future Selina Kyle asks. She holds a large hunting knife so naturally it seems like an extension of herself.

Down the alley a ways something clangs and the

three in pursuit and the one being pursued hear whispered cussing. The three immediately sprint in that direction and Hunter doesn't hesitate, unfurling himself from the fetal position between the dumpster and the wall, sprinting in the opposite direction though it seems too easy. He curses his genetics under his breath, that he's more Peter Parker than Spiderman. His shoes crunch on broken glass and rain-wet pavement and he's sure they can hear him but he runs anyway. The drunk down the alley bought him a minute, maybe.

He tosses his jacket to the ground and tugs the hood of his sweatshirt up over his head. He ducks into the nearly-deserted metro station—past his curfew, but the hour not so late to justify the emptiness. Rather, this stop has gone neglected, only a matter of time until it's removed from the city budget altogether. Hunter hops the turnstile. No one notices, or cares to intervene. The apathy of humanity at its finest. No matter, security cameras smile over the length of the station in lieu of paying employees to attend to riders and Hunter tips his head up to greet them before lowering it again. *If I'm going to disappear,* he thinks, *I'm leaving behind as much evidence as possible.*

He tucks himself into shadow near the center of the platform, awaiting whatever train rolls through next. He lost his cellphone and the cash he'd just picked up when Future Selina Kyle and her knife had startled him mid-text. If anyone here looked any less terrifying than she, Hunter would ask for help—but this line is more than a few stops from anywhere he should be at this hour, so he waits.

He blames his overly cautious customer who insisted on meeting after curfew in the suburbs to make their transaction, concerned that a handoff at school—despite Hunter's years of experience and lack of getting caught—would be too risky. Test answers would ensure his customer kept his spot as starting quarterback for the upcoming Homecoming game, but getting caught would spell the end of not only his sports tenure, but his academic standing. Of course, reading *To Kill a Mockingbird* hadn't dawned on the boy.

A train. Hunter steps on, not noticing the destination or even the direction: he's so far near the end of the line that odds were good the train was heading where he needed to. A few strangers do the same, though with the confidence granted by having a "where" and a "why" for their late travel that probably didn't involve selling test answers to support their comic book addiction. Hunter moves to the front of the car, planning to exit from a different door than he entered. A woman sits muttering to herself. She smells like soap and cigars. Hunter avoids eye contact, leaning against the wall just out of sight of those they might roll slowly past at subsequent stops, willing himself to shrink into the safety of his hoodie.

The interior lights stay dim. Lamps like streetlights spot the tunnel as the train car careens through, causing a sort of strobe effect. At the next stop a few more people clamor aboard. A priest.

A frazzled mother with too many grocery bags, an infant, and a small, bleary-eyed child up past his bedtime. The little boy whines and she pulls him onto her lap. Hunter contemplates asking for help, but shakes his head. No explanation for him being out past curfew would sate his parents' curiosity and involving other people just ensures his parents find out—the unspoken code of adults. A couple of tired-looking men in suits chatter cheerily about the upcoming office Christmas party that's still months away, annoying the muttering woman who glares at them. They're nearing downtown.

More stops, more passengers on. No one exits, the car is filling up so Hunter uses this time to make eye contact with as many people as he can, willing an imprint of his face to burn into their memory. He figures his odds of being helped are better before he explains to everyone just what he was doing out at nearly midnight on a school night. No one wants to rescue the kid who sells test answers and essays to classmates, a brainiac delinquent, and the anxiety of coming up with a suitable lie doesn't hold up against the option of remaining silent. Without a reason as to why those three were after him, he can't be certain that being safe now means he's safe in the future—so he needs people to see him, remember him. The priest. The mother. The businessmen.

Maybe he's read too many comics, seen too many movies, he thinks as he nears a fringe down-town stop with a hoard of passengers-to-be waiting. At the other end of the car a gaggle of riders crowd, eager to get off. He doesn't have time to join them before they stop, so he moves to the door nearest him and steps out. He barely has time to feel the concrete of the platform under his shoe when the entire tunnel rumbles and erupts into chaos.

The sound is so loud that Hunter cringes involuntarily at the edge of the platform, near the door he just stepped out of. People sprint past him. Screams rise from where the explosion occurred, making the epicenter of the chaos easy to spot.

One of the cars ahead of his has been consumed by flames. Strong arms tug Hunter upwards and away from the platform's edge. He's grateful that someone else has the focus-during-crisis skills he's exhausted for the night—until rough cloth is placed over his mouth and nose. The flames, the tunnel, the train all slip from view.

"Limp! Pretend you're injured," a strangely accented voice hisses to someone. The Foreigner.

Then he hears her, Future Selina Kyle. "My brother! He's been hurt!"

Her voice drops to a whisper, each hard *k* punctuated by slight breath. "Here kitty kit—"

Then nothing.

Now

PACE OUTSIDE THE CLOSED DOOR OF THE COUNCIL chambers. Even with the heightened hearing of a predator I can hear nothing beyond it. Caius leans against the cool basement wall, arms crossed at his chest, eyes closed. He has been a comfort these past few nights in Zeke's absence, even offering to escort me to the Council. Since being summoned I've thought of nothing else. Perhaps the distraction from my loss should be a comfort, though I struggle to think of it as such.

"Calm yourself, child."

I shake my head. "What do they want with me?"

"I've told you, they wish to speak with you about Zeke's passing. Nothing more. You act like you've done something wrong."

"Then why does it feel like I'm on trial?"

He doesn't answer. I know we will not be disturbed, as the entrance to this section of the hotel is private, owned and maintained by the sect and considered a safe place for Keepers to conduct business. The oldest hotel in the city and still it doesn't rival a single member of the Council in age or grace. The sect spares no expense in its upkeep or revitalization. Like most beautiful, old things, the elegance must outlive the threat of becoming threadbare or dingy or obsolete. Even this section survives, mahogany paneling and chandeliers impeccably maintained, fresh flowers adorning the small antique tables to either side of the door—their brightness oddly juxtaposed against the macabre art one might expect in a place where vampires meet.

I pause in front of one such painting. A woman

wearing bloodied tatters and covered in faint traces of Nordic tattoos wears a raven headdress, all skull and feathers. She stands in a battlefield at night, the ground covered in recently dead. The only things in the painting not marred by battle and blood are the sword and shield she holds. Her eyes glow faintly, as does the aura around her. A wisp of light trails from one of the corpses to the blade of her sword.

"Beautiful, isn't she?" a voice erupts in the quiet, startling me.

I turn. A man dressed in a suit that reminds me of the 1920s and who smiles as easily as Gatsby stands in front of a now-yawning door. Inside I see a large round table, ornately carved of the same mahogany that gleams in the rest of the hotel.

"A powerful myth, the Valkyries," he adds.

I nod, studying him before continuing. "Zeke spoke of them to me, a long time ago. He told me that there's rumor of a secret faction of female Everlasting who champion different beliefs than the Keepers or the Praedari."

"You speak more eloquently than I would have guessed."

"When it suits me," I challenge.

The corners of his mouth turn up, though I hesitate to call it a smile. "I am sure your Usher told you more than that, child. Ezekiel Winter chased after rumors as though they were the Holy Grail. His methods were unorthodox, but the Council cannot question his efficacy or dedication."

"Did he find them?" I ask.

"More rumors to distract himself with, or the Valkyries?"

"The Valkyries."

"You would know better than I, child, what he did or did not find. But the thing about seeking the Holy Grail when you're one of the Everlasting—we are already eternal. It becomes less about the object you seek and more about the story. In this case," he shrugs, "the story is all of it."

"That's what you've summoned me here for, a story, haven't you?" I ask carefully. I do not know what Zeke told them about me, just that he kept the secret of my visions from most and cautioned that I do the same.

"We've summoned you for the truth, Delilah. Come now, meet the Council." He places his hand on the small of my back in a too-familiar way and guides me towards the door. Caius steps towards us. The man raises a hand. "She must do this alone."

"She is my ward. I swore an oath."

"And there's nowhere safer than in Council chambers. I assure you no blood will be spilled behind these doors tonight. You may wait here if you like," he says, his voice edged in something dangerous despite gesturing to some seating as a concierge might. Caius grunts and stands against the wall near the door, arms crossed. I have no doubt that no matter how long I am inside I will find him still standing sentinel when I return.

Inside, seven high-back leather chairs surround a circular mahogany table. Two seats empty. The other five seat people I've never seen before but I can guess their importance. The chairs, the table— the only Everlasting allowed into Council chambers are invited guests and even that is a rare occurrence. Trials take place elsewhere—somewhere, I imagine, where sunlight could never reach and screams could never be heard. Salons, business meetings, and celebrations spill into other rooms of the seemingly infinite hotel, reaching even as far as the lobby where Caius waits. Even Zeke likely never more than glimpsed this room.

Everyone stares as I enter and I glance to the man, unsure of what to do. He gestures to a vacant seat near the door, one of the seven.

"Forgive our arrangement—it's not often we have visitors," he says, taking the other vacant seat. A woman across from me smirks as I sit in the chair. I glance at the expressions of the others, but besides her smirk and the plastered-on smile of the man who fetched me from the lobby, these people could be statues.

"First of all," the man begins, "we wish to extend

our condolences at your loss. The death of your Usher is a loss deeply felt by the sect. He—"

The smirking woman rolls her eyes.

"He didn't *die*," I interject before I can stop myself from arguing the semantics of a predator. I know what the Council thinks—that Zeke met his end at the hand of another predator, perhaps in a dispute for territory or prey or because he found himself too deep into whatever great mystery he might have been after at the time, the Valkyries or another. They do not think him *murdered*, they think him *dead*—you don't consider a bear murdered by another bear in the wild. Murder is premeditated, motivated. Everything, even the Everlasting, *dies*, and usually at the hand of another, but that alone does not require it be *murder*. The definition lies not in the effect, but in the cause.

A palpable silence and I notice the air shifting around even the stoic members of the Council, a tension as when the quarry realizes they're being stalked. I've spoken out of turn. I've contradicted something they know to be true. I'm alone with the wolves and even if Caius burst through that door any one of the Elders seated at this table could ash me before he understood what was happening.

"Delilah," the man begins carefully, "I know this loss must come as a shock, but Ezekiel Winter is dead. The Everlasting do not leave corpses, but I assure you—"

"I know he's *dead*. I'm saying he didn't *die*. He was murdered."

Again the palpable silence, but it quickly dissolves to whispering. The smirking woman narrows her eyes at me.

"That's a bold claim, child," she hisses. "The punishment for killing another Everlasting comes from the Ritae Aequitas. Those practices have been dormant for centuries and to levy such a grave accusation—"

"The punishment for killing another Everlasting *if you're caught*," an attractive man next to the smirking woman retorts. "How naïve can you be?

Don't leave a survivor to tattle," the attractive man adds, shrugging.

"Let her speak freely, Evelyn," a woman with a honeyed voice next to me says, addressing the smirking woman who now glares at the man next to her. "Please, Delilah, continue."

"Enough!" The man who brought me inside slams his fist on the table. "Decorum matters in these chambers. We are not *Praedari*." This last word drips the venom with which it was meant. The quarreling Elders quiet.

"That is better. Now, introductions. I am Leland. Though we do not have assigned positions within the Council, we do each fill a role that plays to our strengths. I tend to play host when we have visitors. This," he gestures to the formerly smirking woman, "is Evelyn, something of an occultist and historian. If the sect has a secret, she is its keeper." Though his tone is light, she looks displeased at this last statement, her lips pursing. She's dressed sensibly, as you might expect someone named Evelyn who is an occultist and historian to dress: neutral colors, hair pulled back in a bun, minimal jewelry except a pin on her lapel that bears some crest I don't recognize.

"This is Alistair." Leland gestures to a man who appears to have been uncharacteristically old when he had his Becoming, gray peppering his hair. He, too, wears a suit, the unspoken dress code amongst male members of the Council, though his pocket kerchief and tie stand out amongst the predominantly neutral palette of the Council in the seemingly ever-shifting shades of a peacock. My attention falls to his wrists: platinum cufflinks in the style of tiny maps adorn his wrists. "Alistair is responsible for curating the majority of the gallery you saw in the lobby."

"They're from my personal collection," he boasts.

"I found the Valkyrie particularly enthralling," I respond, clearly speaking out of turn again.

He smiles the sort of smile that really isn't. "Of

course you did. It's a shame the artist went mad and never painted another. She showed so much potential . . . " His tone leads me to believe that *went mad* is a politesse for my benefit, that her fate may have been at the hands of the subject of her painting if, indeed, some of the darker rumors Zeke gathered about the Valkyries were correct.

"Next we have Brantley," Leland continues, interrupting more politely than seems possible. His voice takes on a slight edge, though, as he continues. "Our resident chameleon—far older than he presents himself, he's learned to adapt with the times rather than, as he would tell you, cling to outdated traditions and mannerisms that no longer serve the sect." The latter half of this statement sounds tired, as if this verbal battle has waged for years. Brantley, the attractive man, leans back in his chair, arms crossed over his chest. Another suit, though I notice on the back of his chair loops the strap of a leather messenger bag. On his wrist a watch easily recognizable as expensive; gaudy, even.

He shrugs. Whatever nerve Leland hoped to strike, he seems to have missed. Leland doesn't seem to be alone in his dislike of Brantley; Alistair and Evelyn have done little to hide their disgust with him.

That sweetly-lilted voice chimes in and nearly immediately the tension dissolves. "And I am Temperance Cordelia Stafford."

"Yes," Leland continues, regaining his control of introductions. "Not all of us have given up our proper names to the shadows."

Temperance wears a gown that complements Alistair's tie and kerchief, shades of the peacock and far too elegant for a gathering such as this—though you'd never guess by how she carries herself. Her hair falls to the middle of her back, curly, some of it pulled high on her head into an updo secured with what might be diamond-encrusted combs. The light refracting dances on the ceiling whenever she shifts in her seat or turns her head. She wears no other jewelry save for a ring on her left ring finger, where one would wear an engagement ring. The stone is a large, almost cloudy opal. Despite wearing no visible makeup, her skin seems to glow from within. Even her cheeks bear a blush difficult for the Everlasting to fake. I find it hard to take my eyes off her once I've begun studying her. I blink hard and force my gaze to follow Leland's.

His attention falls on a man I didn't notice until now, though he must have been here the entire time. Unlike the other men, he wears grayish what-can-best-be-described-as robes, regal but simple. He has not spoken once, his jaw set, his gaze unflinching. His eyes are gray, how the opal in Temperance's ring looks at certain angles. How had I never noticed him staring at me?

"And this is Enoch, the Eldest among us."

Leland offers no further introduction of the venerable, imposing figure, instead nodding to me to make my address.

"I am Delilah, Childe of Ezekiel Winter, Grandchilde of Ismae the—"

"Naming a Praedari Elder in your address to the

Council of Keepers? Your Usher should have taught you better," Alistair fires.

"With all due respect, Elder—" as Leland says, decorum matters and what is decorum but appearances? "—She is older than both our sects and for me not to name her in the recitation of my lineage would have been dishonest." Return fire. The Germans have a word for Alistair. *Backpfeifengesicht*: a face in dire need of a fist.

Evelyn gives me a curt nod of approval.

"I say where there's the blood of a traitor there's treacherous seed—"

"Do not finish that sentence, Alistair," Evelyn warns.

I notice a couple half-glances in Temperance's direction, her posture erect as she draws herself even more so with a subtle arching of the back, her breasts rising almost imperceptibly, followed by her shoulders. The predator within me flicks tail, recognizing the alertness of that within her. Her tight-lipped smile does little to hide that her cuspids have elongated in response to something I've apparently missed.

"Am I on trial for loyalty to the sect?" I challenge, out of turn, perhaps more hostility to my tone than I originally intended, my tongue flicking like my Beast's tail. "Is Zeke? Why else should my Bloodline be questioned? Surely it is not news to the Council, my lineage."

"Absolutely not, Delilah. We are aware of your lineage. You are here because your Usher spoke often of you—and your gift," Temperance purrs, having dismissed that which rose within her just a second ago. When she speaks, I feel myself involuntarily calm, my Beast retreating to someplace deep inside to slumber for a little while. I suspect hers is a gift of the Blood, as others visibly relax as well.

"Temperance . . ." Leland warns.

"No. She has a right to know that we know her secret. She has a right to know why she was really summoned."

Leland pauses a moment before continuing.

"Very well. Delilah, Temperance is right. Zeke spoke to the Council about your oracular visions. Some"—he glances at Brantley and then to Alistair—"do not believe in such things. They assume knowledge claimed to have been gained this way must have come about from another source. Regardless, it is the duty of the Council to consider all possible sources of information when it comes to sect security."

"Sect security?" Many seconds pass and no one offers so much as confirmation, so I continue. "So Zeke told you what I saw when he made me?"

Five heads nod. Enoch merely stares in his way. Now that I've noticed him I find it difficult to pull my attention elsewhere. Probably what the hunted feel like once they discover they're being stalked.

"Do you remember what you saw that night?" Temperance asks.

I nod. I'm speaking before my brain can intervene and tell my mouth not to. "Sometimes things are hazy but it usually comes back to me later.

That night I saw a pale woman, sleeping but with a thick tube down her throat." The room wavers in my vision and I am in that place again. It echoes as I speak in two places at once. "The tube is clear and filled with red. She is bound at the wrists and ankles with industrial-looking chains. Time passes. I don't know how long. Her eyes open. I feel her hunger . . ."

I become aware of a hand on my arm, startling me from my remembrance and back to the present. My fangs have extended and my pulse races, my Beast again just underneath the skin of this fragile shell. I don't know why I didn't mention the teenagers also sleeping with IVs in their arms, but something in me isn't ready to trust these strangers with the whole of my secret.

"That's roughly what Zeke recounted to us. Is there anything else you remember? Details about the location? Was anyone else present?" Temperance leads in such a way that I suspect at least she knows the answer.

I lie, shaking my head to indicate no. Easier to lie without relying on words. "It's not a linear thing. I—I can't explain it."

"Ssshhh, child. You've done well," she purrs. She stands and offers me her hand. The others stand, too, taking their cue silently. Apparently we are finished. She guides me to the door.

"Wait. Delilah," a voice from the table interrupts. Brantley. "You said Zeke was murdered?"

I nod.

"How do you know?"

"I watched him die."

Before

*N*IGHTTIME BEHIND A DONUT SHOP AND SOME *seedy dive bar. The alley smells like dough and the stink of garbage baked to the bottom of a dumpster by summer. A few backs of heads bob along in the distance towards a car. Three or four or two or eight, the uncertainty one feels in a hall of mirrors. As they start the engine of a black car, dark liquid—the kind of inky dark that makes the shadows themselves—drips into what first resembles a pool of shadow underneath where the engine roars to life, then coagulates and morphs into the shape of a large, dark bird, as if the bird itself melts from underneath the body of*

the vehicle, a bird cast of molten metal and shadow.
I blink and it lands on the dumpster a few feet away.

I turn to go to my car and someone stands in front
of the dumpster, cloaked in shadow. They speak but
the black bird starts cawing so I cannot hear. I see
the glimmer of metal in their hand. It drips light.
Everything drips, but drips as if time has slowed, each
drop peeling off the source and hovering just too long
before plinking below.

I speak but not words, just voice. Zeke's voice.

The figure steps forward but shadow seems to follow
and obscure their features—no, not obscure: the figure
is shadow, either born of it or built of it. One moment
they tower over me, the next I could crouch to be at
their height. How shadows grow and shrink as the sun
moves across the sky. The metal in their hand seems
almost alive, flickering as if reflecting phantom candle-
light. The figure raises the metal which is now wood.
More speaking, drowned out by the bird, but with the
cadence of a prayer.

My eyes widen as I step outside myself. Zeke falls

to his knees, gasping, before slumping to the ground, a hole in his chest where his heart, in life, once beat. The figure erupts into hundreds of black birds, all cawing, cawing, and the cawing is my screaming. The moon, now red, resembles a heart. My screams settle into silence.

Now

"That's it? *That has her convinced it was* murder? A bad dream?" I hear Brantley challenge as Leland gives Temperance a little wave. She escorts me from the room into the lobby with the paintings, her arm linked with mine as sisters might. Before the door closes I hear Evelyn admonish Brantley for being a close-minded dolt incapable of understanding any of the subtleties of our Blood. I'm starting to like her.

Temperance turns to me. "You're worried, but I believe you, Delilah. Zeke and I were close."

I raise an eyebrow.

"Not close like the two of you were, but he came to me shortly after he made you. He didn't know what to share with the rest of the Council. Why did you leave out the teenagers you saw?"

I shrug. "I'm not sure. I just—"

"Wasn't sure who you could trust?"

I nod.

"That's why I didn't press it. But the person who killed him . . . ?"

I shake my head. I really don't know. "What now?"

"Now Caius will escort you home where you'll wait to be summoned again," she says, indicating him with her eyes. "And the Council will argue about what your vision means, where else the information may have come from, whether you can be trusted, and what to do from here. Delilah," her voice softens, "don't take this the wrong way, but . . . don't expect much, okay? You've done your part and Ezekiel would be proud. You didn't let them bully you. You met your duty with grace."

She leans in and gives me an awkward hug, too familiar for us having just met. I manage a weak smile and nod as she disappears into the room pulling the door behind her.

"You sassed off in the Council chambers, didn't you?" Caius asks, grinning. We start walking.

"What? Why would you ask me that?"

"I've known both you and Temperance long enough to know what 'You didn't let them bully you' means."

"I recited my lineage as etiquette dictates when meeting someone for the first time."

"That's an outdated custom and you know it."

I shrug. "It certainly got a rise out of Alistair."

"You were testing them?"

I nod.

"And then Temperance came to your rescue?"

I nod again, noticing the newspaper rolled into a tube in his hand.

"You must've learned that from Zeke," he muses before continuing. "You can't trust her."

"I know."

"I mean it. They start wars. Her kind could convince the Pope he's Jeffrey Dahmer."

"That's an obscure cannibal reference."

"Delilah." There's an edge to his voice. He pauses at the bottom of the stairs.

"I get it, really. I don't trust anyone, except you."

Satisfied, he climbs a few stairs.

"By the way, who says 'ward' anymore?" I call up after him. "Are you in a Jane Austen novel or something?"

Now

"SHE HAS NO IDEA THAT THE ELDER FROM HER vision on the night of her Becoming is her Usher's Usher?" Alistair asks.

"Seems that way," Leland agrees.

"And she somehow didn't see the face of Zeke's supposed murderer? And that some stupid bird drowned out what they talked about?" Brantley's voice still drips with doubt.

"It's likely she did see but can't remember," Evelyn explains, taking on the role of lecturer. "Visions of this nature are incomplete at best. She is lucky she remembers anything of them after they've passed. And the bird . . . the bird could be a symbol rather than a literal bird."

"A symbolic bird? Sounds like a load of symbolic—"

"Question the girl's motives, if you will, but only a fool challenges the existence of something based on their own limited experience."

"Are you making a case for God?" he retorts.

"I'm telling you that we have no idea just what our Blood is capable of. Even the eldest among us"—she glances to Enoch before continuing—"contains multitudes of untapped potential. If we focused our effort and resources on studying the Blood and training those we Usher in maximizing their Gifts, the Everlasting would be revered *as* Gods."

"I could stand to be worshipped." Brantley leans back in his chair, propping his feet up on the large mahogany table, ankles crossed. Sighs and snorts of disgust greet Temperance as she returns to the Council chambers.

"What did I miss?"

"Just Brantley being himself." Leland quips.

"Nothing, got it."

"And your conversation with the girl?" Alistair asks.

"She admitted there was more to her vision." Temperance begins carefully. Enoch can tell she chooses not to reveal something, but Enoch will bide his time. Each body at this table hides more somethings than history textbooks. Alistair is not so tactful.

"More to her vision? What are you withholding, siren?"

Temperance ignores him. "Do you blame her? She has never met us before now. She just lost someone she cares immensely for. I could feel her grief." She pauses, looking to each face for dramatic effect. "Not to mention, well . . . she's the seeker's Childe. How long did he keep her a secret from us? A trusting nature does not run in her blood."

"Which is why she can't be trusted. Treachery—"

He backs off when Evelyn fires a look in his direction that could stop even the tides. "You know where I'm going with this and you know I'm right . . . "

"Delilah had a point, Alistair. Ismae the Bloody predates both of our sects."

"And she still chose a side when the battle came."

"*Chose* a side? She *was* a side." Brantley, in a rare moment of hubris, chimes in. "They don't call her 'the Bloody' for nothing."

Silence blankets the bickering Elders, all children with too many opinions and no discipline. They have ignored Enoch's presence until now, prattling on in their way. Now, one by one, their attention turns to him. Enoch needn't speak for himself. Instead he looks to Leland. Leland makes a fine mouthpiece and, as the youngest, his voice remains the easiest to borrow. He and the others won't notice. Not a gift of the blood, but one learned with time and discipline: ventriloquism, in a manner of speaking.

"We've lost sight of the matter at hand. What of Ezekiel's death?"

"*If* he was murdered," Brantley begins, "it isn't a mystery by whom."

"So you believe the girl?" Alistair asks.

"I said *if.*"

"We all know that *if* isn't in your vocabulary."

Brantley shrugs. "If it was an act of terrorism by the Praedari, I won't be the vote that prevents the Council from defending the sect."

"How patriotic."

"Besides, it's been rather dull these past few decades." Brantley yawns, emphasizing his point.

"That's the appropriately short-sighted reason we've all come to expect."

"And what if her vision tells of her grief and not what came to pass?" Temperance asks.

"Just a minute ago you were championing her." Brantley challenges.

"I'm not saying that she is lying. Not at all, actually. I'm saying she hasn't been shown a face. We cannot be certain who killed Zeke or if he met his end because he dug too far into something none of us knew about."

"Like Temperance, I believe her. I watched her when she told us of Zeke's death. She went elsewhere, retreated to somewhere in her mind." Evelyn explains. "But that matters little to what we must decide."

"Matters little? If Delilah knows more than she's let on—" Alistair argues.

"*If.* But we can't know that. We can sit on our hands and do nothing—as we have for far too long, might I add—or we make moves and punish Zeke's beloved if indeed we unearth her deceit. Either way we can find a way to keep her useful while our investigation of her continues."

"That's the most sense you've spoken in a quarter of a century . . . " Alistair grumbles. Brantley shrugs at the back-handed compliment.

Leland stands. "I call for a vote by the Council of Keepers on the matter of Ezekiel Winter's death.

Thumbs up if we treat his murder as a declaration of war against our sect. Thumbs down if we do not pursue this matter until further evidence is brought to our attention."

Enoch does not vote. He does not need to. Five will vote and there will be no tie. Everything unfolds exactly as it must.

19

Now

"HOW LONG WILL THEY DELIBERATE?" I CALL from the bathroom as I change into shorts and a tank top for bed.

"As long as they need to. And then longer to make sure you squirm," Caius answers matter-of-factly, holding out a mug from which steam rises and curls. I fling myself onto the bed with a sigh and take the mug, enjoying the sharp pain as I wrap my palms around the hot ceramic.

"So I'm a prisoner until then?"

"That's one way of looking at it."

A space feels very different when you're confined

to it, even if it served as a sanctuary before. The walls inch closer to one another. The carpet sucks at your feet like thick mud. The air thickens as you breathe viscosity. I fight the urge to gasp. Sometimes slipping into a vision feels this way: the mind turned from sanctuary to prison.

"There were only six Elders," I say, lifting my head to look up at him.

"I noticed that when the charlatan escorted you inside. More than likely one of them couldn't take time away from personal matters to attend, or perhaps, like Zeke, they don't always make themselves easy to find." He pauses, pretending to study the thick curtains as he draws them shut for me out of habit. "Or perhaps one Slumbers."

I consider this for a moment. Zeke told me that sometimes Elders choose to enter into a deep sleep-like state called the Slumber. In doing so, they become vulnerable to their environment, entirely unable to protect themselves or awaken on their own. Why they make this choice varies, but it is not without reason—going to ground after earning the ire of too-powerful an enemy, loneliness, to wait out a plague or the Inquisition. Rumor has it that most will lock themselves away deep below the earth's surface, guarded by servants Ushered for this very purpose. I never knew whether to believe Zeke or whether it was a bogeyman story told to young Everlasting to keep them in check. Behave, lest ye Elders rise up and reclaim what is rightfully theirs—or something.

"You should rest. They will not summon you tonight and you look drained." He settles into the overstuffed chair next to the bed as he speaks, adjusting a pillow to support his neck.

"I am, actually. More so than usual." I close my eyes and for just a second I can smell spice and wood.

"Did you force a vision?" He asks, concerned.

"No, nothing quite like that," I half-lie. I slipped into what Zeke and I called The Remembrance, but I didn't force anything. Though his concern comes from a genuine place, I don't feel too badly about my lie of omission.

"Well, Temperance is a *vampire* as well as one of the Everlasting," Caius jokes. "That's probably why you're so tired."

I smile at his cleverness—rare is the Keeper that allows themselves to be called a vampire, believing it to demean the superiority of their nature. *Everlasting,* though, has a more elegant ring to it, maintains a distance from the gritty reality, and adds a certain air of grace and dignity that the Praedari feel little need to replicate. No, the Praedari fancy themselves the ultimate predator: vampires.

"You needn't sleep in that chair," I invite as I roll towards one side of the bed and shimmy underneath the comforter. "The bed is big enough for the both of us. I'll even keep my clothes on," I add just to make him uncomfortable.

He considers my invitation for just a moment before shaking his head "no." My joke seems lost on him. "This serves me well enough, thank you. We sleep like the dead regardless where."

Now

"**I**'M GOING OVER TO JOSH'S TO WORK ON OUR English project," Logan calls over his shoulder, having just shoveled mashed potatoes and roast into his mouth and loaded his dirty plate into the dishwasher.

"For *Pride and Prejudice* which you have yet to finish?" His stepmother teases between bites, indicating an untouched copy of the novel still on the counter.

Logan smiles and offers a shrug, scooping up the book.

"It's not my fault they can't assign the *cool*

version of it, the one with the zombies." He pauses at the door. "Hey—how late did you say dad was working?"

"Probably about one. He's in court tomorrow so it'll be a late night for him. Why?"

"You know, I could have Josh come here to work on the project. Then you wouldn't have to be alone."

She waves Logan off. "I appreciate that, but I'm fine. It's going to be a late night for me, too." She holds up her coffee mug for emphasis. "My thesis committee wants a polished draft by Thanksgiving. I'm about to cause the town a coffee shortage."

"Alright . . . "

"Really, I'm fine. Nothing interesting ever happens around here, you know that," she adds lightly, smiling.

"Okay," he nods, convinced. "Love you, mom."

"Love you, too. Watch out for zombies!"

⟱

Josh is one of those kids whose parents inexplicably whisked them away to the country, onto a beautiful acreage that used to support a hobby farm—only to keep him enrolled in Logan's school and make the forty-five minute drive twice a day. Their loyalty extends beyond the school district to include restaurants, salons, mechanics, coffee shop, the library, and even pet grooming boutiques—despite there being two small towns along the way that, combined, boast at least one very pared-down version of most of these. Their new favorite hobbies are complaining about this drive and brainstorming about what they might use the hobby farm *for*, if only they had the time. (Which they might if they didn't drive an hour and a half for work, dinner, a haircut, an oil change, a latte, to return books, or get their toy cockapoos bathed and trimmed.) Of course, Josh being on the team with Logan further complicates his daily routine, so often he stays at Logan's place; Logan tries to make the drive out to his place when he can't. Logan's known Josh since they were both about five. He shared his Twinkies with Logan, which is also pretty much how Logan's girlfriend won him over a couple years ago.

The snow's been holding out, so right now the drive is easy. Logan likes driving in the country: there are speed limits but it's so rare to run into another person out here that they really are more of a suggestion than a hard-and-fast rule. The roads out here curve gently, so gently that no sign is posted warning of them or urging motorists to slow down. Of course, had they once been posted they'd likely all have been stripped during senior prank week each year. That little act of defiance counted as street cred in these parts. Despite it being chilly, he lets down the front driver window and turns the radio up. Something Top 40, but he doesn't care.

He's singing along to Taylor Swift when he notices headlights in his rearview mirror. The road stretches on fairly straight here, so he's not sure how he didn't notice another vehicle until now. He slows just a little before he realizes they're going at least as fast as he is, so he pays them little mind. Like driving in the winter around here, the greater danger comes from the other person not knowing what they're doing. Someone driving as fast as he does out here means they know the landscape, too, each pothole, each divot mapped permanently in their mind.

Their headlights grow larger, less distinct, brighter in the mirrors as they cut through the darkness. Logan takes his usual turn onto Willard Creek Road only to be followed by the same set of headlights. Having slowed down for the turn, he keeps a slower pace. It's not a popular road. None of the roads out here are unless you're a tractor or a cow that's somehow escaped the fence at the property line. What were Josh's parents thinking?

The headlights, however, haven't taken his cue and slowed, nor sped up to pass him, the car still careening behind him at a dangerous clip. They flash their brights a couple times and he's reminded of an urban legend about a gang initiation game where soon-to-be gang members will drive with their headlights off so cars will blink theirs as a courtesy. Doing so marks these good Samaritans, as the initiates will then drive these cars off the road and shoot everyone inside.

Never mind that *they* flash their brights at *him*: trains of thought are not always logical and all he can think of are the news report Logan and his stepmom watched before dinner, violent accounts of vandalism taken too far in cities far larger than theirs, mandatory curfews being considered, all possibly gang-related or so the newscasters like to conjecture. It's not like people can play this game in the city, so what's the next tactical choice? The suburbs. Even better: the country surrounding the suburbs. He glances to his phone on the seat next to him, but before he can decide to call—who?—the car pulls into oncoming traffic's lane, so close Logan can almost feel the vibration of their horn when they start honking it. He pulls off to the side, onto the gravel shoulder, heart racing. The other car doesn't slow. The honking doesn't stop.

Logan is bathed in light as they cut close, kicking up gravel that pings off metal. A rush of air and flurry of noise—honking echoed by laughter—as the car whooshes past. He recognizes the borrowed Mustang from the rear just as his phone beep-beeps on the seat next to him. A text message.

Party out at Old Mill Road! Tiffany Lang.

Tiffany Lang out to a party on a Wednesday night, and Logan doubts her mother knows she has her daddy's ride. He laughs to himself, more to shake off rattled nerves than because of Tiffany Lang's stunt. Someone's getting a sheep's eye from the biology supply closet in their Nalgene bottle tomorrow, he plots.

"Come on, Logan, pull yourself together," he chuckles to no one. Okay, maybe not a sheep's eye.

That's when he notices just how bright the interior of his car has become, the dashboard illuminated to an eerie glow, indistinguishable from the windshield, from the rearview mirror. Screeching of tires on pavement, sickening crunch of metal-on-metal. The force of the seatbelt in his pelvis or the impact itself knocks the wind out of him as the airbag hits him in the face or his face hits the airbag before snapping back against the headrest. A warm tickle on his forehead, but he's aware that he's aware.

With some difficulty he manages to push the driver's side door open, fumble with his seatbelt until it clicks free. He falls to his knees on the ground, where gravel shoulder meets worn pavement, breathing heavily. Everything hurts. Sharp pain radiates up and down from his left knee where he can see a bruise already forming. Hot tears form in his eyes.

He hears car doors close, shoes on pavement. Voices arguing.

"Was ramming the car really necessary? What if he'd died?"

"Yeah, maybe you don't remember, but mortals aren't like us. They can't survive this kind of thing."

"She's right. We need him alive. He's no good to us dead."

"Lighten up, guys. He's fine, see?"

"I think we lose points for damaging them," the first voice offers.

"Oh, like you think Pierce's pack isn't going to rough them up? That ugly brute Johnny can't *resist* a fight and Lydia doesn't carry that knife for show, trust me. Who've they got on their list? That Kiley girl and some guy named Hunter?"

"What's this one's name?"

The four voices now tower over Logan. One booted foot nudges him in the ribs, punctuating the question.

Logan tries to speak but can only manage a guttural "uhhhhnnnnn . . ."

21

Now

CAIUS RETURNS FROM HUNTING TO INFORM ME THE Council has summoned me once again, as promised. I take extra care getting dressed, pulling my hair back off my face. I fold a sheathed dagger into my jacket.

"That's from the raid?" he asks, though it's less of a question and more of an observation.

"You recognize it?" I say with some surprise and he nods. Though he claims to have been present for the raid, I'm not sure what role he played. Was he inside the warehouse? Did he help Zeke put all the pieces in place beforehand? Did he keep to the shadows and pick off Praedari as they hunted?

The plan was a trap, a raid on an alleged Keeper cell within Praedari territory to be orchestrated by Zeke—at least, until another Keeper operative infiltrating a pack was discovered, their cover blown. Zeke couldn't save the operative, but since the timing was fortuitous with the approach of one of their sacred nights, Zeke convinced our pack to host the next gathering. The Rite of Howling, celebrated at the full moon, always culminated with a symbolic, albeit lethal, hunt symbolizing the Praedari's dominance over the Keepers. Usually a Praedari brother or sister honored their sect by acting as tribute, but what luck that my first Howling be with a true-to-life Keeper and this tradition could be honored with an *actual* Keeper sacrifice!—or such was the ruse. So with the assistance of the Council—in the form of equipment and keeping the media at bay, not *actually* getting their hands bloody—we were able to execute the entire pack we'd been infiltrating and take down many of the members of those packs visiting for the rite.

Though we called the initial plan "the raid" because Zeke had planned for it to be a raid on a made-up Keeper cell within Praedari territory, the name stuck because of how we cornered them in a warehouse and picked them off like—well, that was neither the first nor the last time I almost saw my Final Moment, a story for another time.

Caius starts to explain. "He pulled it off Tomas, by all reports a loudmouth piece of . . . Well, you know. You met them all. Zeke grew rather fond of him, said his loyalty was unmatched by any he'd met. Leave it to Zeke to bond with the enemy and then feel no remorse in decimating them." He chuckles, a hoarse sound. "I guess he recovered it to honor him."

A gift for his beloved. I remember what Zeke told me, about our Blood having far greater capacity for affection than other Everlasting. No doubt he felt genuine fraternity with the pack he infiltrated and mourned their deaths, a secret he took to his Final Moment. The curse wrapped within the blessing. I slide an antique six-shooter into a thigh holster underneath my skirt and clasp a pendant—another gift from Zeke—around my throat.

"The Stone of Nyx? Are you sure that's a good idea?"

"You act like I'm bringing a grenade full of sunlight into Council chambers," I joke.

"It's sort of like bringing a wagon full of bloody steaks into a den of starving lions."

"I'm sure it's no secret that I possess the Stone of Nyx. Besides, it's my Bloodright—none of them could attune to it."

"I guess. They may consider it a show of dominance, though."

I shrug. "Maybe it is."

"The gun, though? Even *if* something happened and you opened fire, bullets do about as much as Tic-Tacs."

I smile to myself, remembering something Zeke once said.

"Besides, arming yourself makes you look guilty," Caius offers from the chair.

"I'd rather have one and not need it than need it and not have one," I explain.

"Isn't that from a movie?"

"Yeah."

"The woman that says that line dies, doesn't she?"

"Yeah," I shrug.

Before

"**I** ALREADY TOLD YOU THAT I'VE MADE MY DECIsion. You're not going to change my mind." I reach for my six-shooter but Zeke has already grabbed it.

"A gun? You might as well pelt her with gumballs, Delilah," he admonishes. "No Everlasting fears bullets." He turns the revolver over in his hands, inspecting it with a faint smile of approval despite his outward skepticism. "Where'd you get this, anyhow?"

"None of your business," I snap, swiping the gun from his hand.

He frowns. "Don't be angry—"

"Don't tell me how to feel."

"I'm only looking out for you."

"You think me incapable."

"You know that's not true."

"Then you don't trust me."

He sighs, rubbing his furrowed brow. "I swear, Delilah, if my hair could gray you'd be the reason." He studies me a moment, frowns, then continues. "Fine."

"Fine?"

He tosses his hands up in surrender. "Fine. You can go in my place."

I smile.

"You're stubborn."

I shrug. "Probably why I survived."

"Probably." In the kitchen he sits at a small square card table and gestures to the other folding chair. "This is a delicate matter, Delilah, not a time for brute force. Simone considers her collection an extension of herself. She won't part with anything easily."

"And theft isn't an option?"

"Impossible, and don't consider that a challenge. No, for this you'll have to convince her to give it up willingly. You've seen me fight, right? And Caius?"

I nod.

"Simone doesn't look like much, but she could ash us both blindfolded with her arms bound behind her back. She didn't just command armies; she Ushered them. She singlehandedly trained them and fought alongside them until her empire was secured. Once it was, she handled the overpopulation with genocide. When the Keepers and Praedari split into factions, she was asked to serve as the Keepers' unofficial warlord. Now she dedicates that same tactical genius to safeguarding her collection."

"Understood."

"We get one chance at this. Others are vying for the same artifact but Simone has decided that instead of awarding it to the highest bidder she'd see what else we're willing to offer. Be careful, Delilah—if you offer your soul she'll find a way to take it."

"What is this artifact, exactly?"

"It's safer that you don't know. She'll know I sent you and what it is I seek."

"And if she takes our payment and sends me back with a decoy?"

Zeke shakes his head. "She should honor whatever agreement you reach. She carries herself like a snake-oil salesman but too many tricks loses business—and blood—and news travels quickly amongst Everlasting. Let me worry about Simone's end of the transaction."

I stand, adjusting the jacket into which I've tucked the revolver. "Got it." I start for the door.

"Delilah—"

I turn at his address.

"For God's sake, take this at least."

He strides to me, the corners of his mouth twitching as if he hides a smile. He pulls something from his pocket. A deep red stone about the size of a quarter dangles from an intricately woven silver chain.

"Here," he says, clasping the pendant around my neck. When the stone meets my décolletage it immediately warms. A quiet hum starts in my ears and slides to my temples, as if it buzzes with electricity. My Beast within raises its head, stirring from slumber.

"It's . . . beautiful."

"The Stone of Nyx, the Greek Goddess of night. Some sources say she alone birthed creation and mothered the twins Sleep and Death, two states we are caught between as Everlasting. She's considered an oracle, just as you are. This pendant belonged to Ismae the Bloody, and now it is yours by Right of Blood."

"Why not yours?"

"I didn't inherit her Gift as you have."

I nod. I feel the predator within me more embodied than usual, as if a part of me has turned a camera inward and the scene unfolds. She circles the heavy stone, eyeing it suspiciously, snarling. The stone pulses in response. I catch Zeke staring, a faint red glow emanating from it for a moment. My Beast growls. The stone burns my flesh, white hot, a sensation I haven't felt since my Binding—and at once cool again, the glow subsiding. My Beast quiets, slinking to the corner of my soul and settling in to slumber.

"Her Blood is your Blood; her rage your rage. The predator within you will accept this dominance in time, though it won't be easy. It is a pendant of transmutation—you will bathe it in your blood each full moon. This will serve to attune it to you, as well as infuse your blood with the blood of those who've worn it before you—including Ismae and, if the stories are true, the Goddess Nyx herself."

"I won't let you down," I offer. Nothing else seems appropriate for a gift of this magnitude.

"You could never let me down, Delilah."

I arrive at the address I'm given, a large mansion on considerable acreage outside of town—very much the type Hollywood would cast as the home of a powerful vampire, with spires and stained glass and a tall, black, wrought iron gate around the estate. Unlike the movies, though, the lawn is pristine and the gate does not creak when I push it open. Topiaries trimmed meticulously, but in simple shapes, dot the landscape as far as I can see. Around the property various flowers bloom, the colors not entirely discernible from a distance at night, mostly darker shades illuminated by meager moonlight. Despite the harsh architecture, the property welcomes visitors.

A woman greets me at the door, gestures for me to come inside.

"Lady Simone will see you in the parlor." Her eyes dart to an archway to the right. My eyes follow and, when I look to her to nod in confirmation, she's already disappeared. My boots click on the marble floor as I cross to and enter the parlor. I eye a gold-and-ivory brocade settee that, though not dusty, has likely been untouched for longer than I've been one of the Everlasting. Like in a museum, nothing feels touchable and yet the urge is overwhelming. I reach out to an urn on an ornate mantle.

"Good evening, Delilah," a voice interrupts my act of defiance and I recoil as though a child caught with my hand in the cookie jar.

"I—"

The woman smiles. She was lovely once, and the half of her face that is not gnarled scar tissue still is. Even sans mirror, her shiny, new skin—puckered, as though she somehow survived a funeral pyre in her final mortal moments, but not unscathed—seamlessly smooths into a less cruel countenance. I do not doubt the seclusion of this estate to be at least somewhat related to her appearance, a truth most unfortunate. For a moment I pity her: in a mirror we'd likely be equally grotesque, the curse unavoidable, but she must live with this disfigurement every day. I want to ask how it happened but I do not.

"Ezekiel sent you, I presume. Had he pressing business to attend to?"

"He did," I lie. "He said you'd know why I'm here."

"Is that—the Stone of Nyx?" She steps closer, jealousy alight in her eyes. I can feel the Beast within her stir, as mine did earlier.

"It is. You know of it?"

"Any Everlasting who appreciates beauty knows of the Stone of Nyx. Bold that you wear it so openly—or perhaps that is what Zeke has sent you to offer?"

"The Stone of Nyx is far more valuable than what my Usher asks of you." I have no idea if that's true, but it's worth a stab.

She takes another step towards me, eyes flashing

like Tolkien's Gollum in the throes of his desire for the One Ring, that same desperation and, in some ways, the sense of innocence that underlies it.

"What is it *you* seek, Delilah?"

"Why don't we see how this goes, first?" I bluff. I have no interest in her collection save what it might yield for my Usher.

"As you wish. I never ask twice. Instead, if you wish to please your Usher and return to him with what he seeks, you will not decline my next request."

༄

After a short drive, Lady Simone and I arrive at a sprawling cemetery. A part of her estate, the mausoleums onsite have been plagued with break-ins and, as she says, "Less than savory nighttime affairs." Everything has a price: this artifact, apparently, being worth exterminating the Praedari pests who've been vandalizing her property. Typical of those in power, to put a price on it rather than get their own hands dirty. Though she fails to elaborate, I can only think of a few reasons to dig up dusty old bones and rotting corpses and none of them are, as she puts it, savory.

"I'll wait here," she says dismissively, pulling out a tablet.

I sigh and roll my eyes, leaving her and the chauffeur in the town car. I stride to the cluster of mausoleums she indicated as being the most recent in a rash of break-ins, a couple city blocks' distance from the parked car. As I approach, I hear voices. I tuck myself into the shadows as I stalk nearer.

I freeze when I am tapped on the shoulder.

"Well aren't you a pretty little thing?" a male voice snickers.

As I turn my head I'm met with a wall of flesh snapping my head back on impact. The blow would've killed a mortal, but instead my Beast within growls, lunging. I am fangs and nails and the tearing of his jugular. No pulse, but I can feel the satisfying wetness, the dark grass made darker as the liquid spreads. I drink. Within seconds he falls into ash.

More hands on me, two, then four, then six, and then a piercing through flesh and muscle and between the ribs that form the bone-cage from which my dead heart sings. My eyes widen. I look to the long shaft of wood in my chest—a classic weapon against our kind, as effective as it is tongue-in-cheek. I glance to the faces which mirror my widened eyes, then again to the stake. I am able to do this a few times before I realize I shouldn't be able to.

"What the—"

"It's glowing!"

"How—"

The shaft of wood works its way from my flesh, the force originating somewhere behind my heart and pushing outward. It hits my foot as it falls, then softly thuds to the grass, a sound beyond mortal ears but as loud as a footfall on a stair in an abandoned house to those of us gathered here. The wound cauterizes as if by a phantom surgeon. The surprise that caught even the predator within off-guard a moment ago subsides and I am on another man in an instant, a blur of fangs and kicking and animalistic cries, one of us indiscernible from the other. I feel sharp jabs landing, cutting, piercing, and then the flesh searing shut each time.

By the time the searing halts and the wounds start to take, I am only vaguely aware of the two figures I trip over as I advance on the last man standing. He pulls a gun and I barely have time to smirk before he fires. I scream as a bullet burns through me. The burning doesn't stop, though, and I feel a sensation like splashing, but internally—not blood, too thin and light and nothing to be blood, as it radiates from the bullet wound in my abdomen.

The man laughs but his laughter stops short as a stake plunges out through his chest towards me and he erupts in a puff of ash. I am pushed to the ground, still screaming.

"Delilah! Are you o—?" But my hand is around the throat of the figure, thinner than the others, choking off the end of the question. I blink a few times and recognize the sickeningly smooth skin on one half of the neck and clarity rushes into my field of vision. I let go, pushing her off and rolling away to survey the wreckage: two piles of ash on blood-darkened grass and two still figures. Simone stands in front of me, rubbing her neck.

"The Stone of Nyx . . . "

The stone, now black and matte, hangs from its silver chain.

"Those two . . . " she says, pointing to the two figures I tripped over.

I stand and reach down to grab the stake from one pile of ash. As I advance on the two figures, eyes still open, I swear I can see the rage of their Beasts within flicker like the last bit of candle flame trying desperately not to be drowned out by wax.

I plunge the stake into the heart of the first figure. Ash. I kneel by the second and plunge the same stake into his heart. Ash.

"I was going to suggest interrogation," Simone says through pursed lips.

"No mercy," I state plainly, wincing as I stand.

"You're hurt."

I look down. Through the dirt and dampness and blood, I see what she means: a mark blazes radially across my abdomen from where I took a bullet, about the size of a baseball, shiny and raw-seeming and familiar. A starburst of new skin, of scar. I glance around to the ash piles. Next to one I see the gun and, though she spots it when I do, I am to it first. I pocket it.

"May I?" She holds her hand out expectantly.

"No," I say, turning and heading back to the car.

I spend the ride refusing to speak, instead tracing the starburst-like pattern on my abdomen.

"He loves me, he loves me not," I silently intone, a children's game that rings as familiar somewhere in distant, untouchable memory. The trick, of course, choosing a flower with an odd number of petals.

You'd think immortality would be as predictable, or would become more so with time—not less. It occurs to me that, until now, I'd never been injured since my Becoming. Never has Zeke let me come to harm. Hurt, of course, being the other side of the same coin: I'd hurt many times, often at Zeke's hands, but always in pursuit of something greater than myself, greater than us. In pain, suffering; in suffering, enlightenment. Unattainable, perhaps, but isn't immortality? Don't we claim that for ourselves out of arrogance?

If Nyx rather than Chaos birthed creation—if she mothered Sleep and Death—who are we to say we've mastered timelessness, as in sleep, or cheated

Death? Aren't we siblings, at best—another phase of the moon that hangs in the night sky? Can one birth without mothering? Can one create without Ushering?

Maybe we place too much importance on the Becoming where instead the grave, or the soil, deserves the credit, for cradling us as the womb from which we emerged the first time, or the worms for showing us the way up. Such could the Praedari question and I was made in their way—so how am I less Praedari than those that I ashed tonight? The rage of Ismae the Bloody sings in my veins, or so a recurring vision often foretells. Zeke repeated as much to me before I left. Her blood, some Praedari thugs, nearly killed me tonight when I thought myself immortal; and yet it was her Blood that saved my life when I thought myself dead.

My grasp on logic becomes tenuous, as when the ground beneath me shifts and gives way to one of these visions. A spiral dances in front of me and I feel its pull, or a vision indeed lurks in my field of reason, awaiting the chance to strike.

The honking of a horn jars me from reverie. The spiral, the vision, these questions will have to wait. After all, I have forever or it has me.

ട്ര

When I enter the apartment Zeke is pacing. I feel his Beast stalking just beneath the surface, further enraged by being given a taste of control before being denied. I promised Simone I would deliver the artifact without gazing upon it myself and, though my curiosity great, I am familiar with the story of Pandora's box: had she just listened she would not have unleashed from that prison such evils on humanity. Better safe than sorry, I figure, as I place the carved wooden box with the velvet lining peeking out on the floor next to the door, one of the few spaces as of yet undestroyed by what I can only guess was a tornado, or burglary, or war.

The bed, flipped on its side, leans against the broken window. Shards of glass litter the floor, trailing to the kitchen, the remaining shrapnel of the window. The bookcase has crashed onto the desk, breaking it in two, but not before nearly every book was either torn in two or flung at the wall, some leaving craters in the drywall. The bathroom sink blocks the doorway to the kitchen. Water pools in the bathroom, the pipes mangled and no longer spewing water.

"You're angry," I say, stepping inside.

"You're hurt," he says, his gaze directed to the scar on my abdomen. "You weren't supposed to get hurt." He shakes his head.

"But you were angry before I walked in the door," I point out.

"Simone called me on the way over," he explains. I must've been lost in thought when she did.

"It doesn't matter," I start. "There it is." I gesture to the box by the door. I offer a proud smile, despite his obvious distress, my attempt at hiding my gloating—my attempt at minimizing the severity of what happened—a failure.

"That woman is insufferable, but not a threat. And, until now, I didn't think her an idiot," he mutters, pacing again.

"What are you talking about?"

He stops, eyes boring into me. "You weren't supposed to get hurt. She and I struck a deal months ago."

I furrow my brow. "You gotta walk me through this, Zeke . . . "

"Simone and I struck a deal for this months ago. She'd already been paid. The entire thing—"

"—was a test," I say flatly. A test-turned-accident, like my Becoming, like so many other things since. A numbness settles in where usually the predator within paces, waiting for an opening.

He nods.

"That's why you gave in so easily about my taking your place," I say, my tone flat.

He nods again.

"So Simone wasn't meant to be a threat at all, isn't an Elder—didn't Usher an entire army—" but he's shaking his head before I can finish.

"The story, everything I told you about Simone is really Ismae's story. Ismae the Bloody Ushered entire armies to secure her empire, then destroyed them—of course, there's more to her story than that."

"Was she not the first Praedari?" I retort, both angry and curious.

"When the Keepers offered Ismae the position of warlord, she declined and instead fought against them. That's the short version, at least. The Praedari look to her as a symbol but I'm not so sure she returns the adoration. She never intended to mother a revolution."

"You speak of her in the present tense . . . " But he doesn't respond. He's calmed some, sitting in the chair which miraculously emerged from the outburst unscathed.

"Come, let me see." He puts his arms out.

I go to him. He crinkles his brow, frowning as he runs his finger over the light pink starburst of scar tissue.

"Does it hurt?"

"Not anymore."

"How did it happen?"

"This," I say, pulling the pistol from my jacket.

He takes it from me, inspecting it. He releases the cylinder, spilling bullets onto his lap. Grabbing one between two fingers, he cusses as his flesh sizzles.

"The Praedari have gotten more clever. These have been blessed. Delilah . . . you should be dead. How did—"

That's when he notices the Stone of Nyx, now matte black. The gravity—the guilt—of what he's done washes over him, nearly palpable. Tears glisten in his eyes, perhaps the first I've seen there and I hear his voice, "Delilah, I—" But I am on him in an instant, my jaw snapping at his throat, fangs extended.

He catches my throat in his hand, easily dropping me to the floor and straddling my chest, pinning my arms above my head until my Beast within recognizes his dominance and slinks to the recesses of where my heart used to beat. I breathe heavily out of habit, coming out of my predatory daze. We'd been here before, more than once, me trying to kill him.

"You're right to be angry—"

"Oh, well, let me thank you for that *permission*," I nearly spit at him.

"But you have to believe that I never meant you to get hurt."

"I know," I grumble, exhausted, limp. I growl out of frustration.

He climbs off me, helping me to my feet. Without another word he takes up the box and I wrap the bullets in a shred of some torn bedsheet from the mess he's made of them on the floor. He makes a call and we head out into the night to hail a cab. A few nights in a hotel while someone fixes the apartment, all signs of the struggle erased except in recent memory. So it's gone and so it goes.

༄

Speaking of erasure, Simone was never heard from again. I asked Zeke about it only once. "Some secrets are best left as ash for the wind to scatter," he responded coolly.

Now

THE WINDING COUNTRY ROAD STRETCHES OUT ahead of her. Nights like these Charlie feels the most like herself, breathing deeply, a chorus of crickets buzzing a lullaby underneath the hum of the engine. She could do this drive with her eyes closed. When Grady called her dad needing a hand, she volunteered. Winter left the electric fences surrounding his property a mess. Since his wife passed he's become a bit of a loner, unwilling to call his own kids back to the farm to help. One time, waist-deep in a tractor older than Charlie, he admitted that his kids just never had what it took to love this place like he did—with his version of this speech punctuated by the clang of metal-on-metal and peppered with all manner of creative cussing.

For as long as she can remember she's flitted between their place and his, fetching tools and parts and working alongside her dad and Old Grady— even when she was young enough that she did more harm than good. She's always been something of a whiz with jury-rigging and, now that she's older, Grady pays her by letting her rummage through the many derelict vintage cars out behind the farmhouse for parts for whatever project she's working on. Really Charlie thinks he enjoys the occasional company, even if they spend some afternoons working side-by-side without saying a word.

She pulls up to the house, each window dark. The glow of fluorescents emanates from the barn where he must be working, making up for time lost trying to mend the fences himself. She hops out of the truck and whistles to herself as she approaches the barn.

"Grady?" she calls, pulling open the heavy door. She's greeted by silence.

Charlie notices a surge of light over-illuminating the interior of the barn through the open door, saturating the room in golden hues before she registers the sound of the explosion behind her. She turns to see the farmhouse erupt in flames. The house she spent nearly as much of her childhood tracking engine sludge throughout as she did her own, blazes against the night sky. She can't breathe for a moment. She's sprinted only a few yards when two figures seem to materialize in front of her. She freezes.

"He's not hurt, but he could get hurt if you cause problems. The choice is yours," a male voice calls.

"Wh—who are you?"

"It doesn't matter. What matters is who *you* are."

"I'm Charlie," she offers defiantly.

"Not your *name*. I don't care about your name. Your name isn't who you are."

"What? Then who the heck am I?" she asks, giving him a long look.

"Some girl we were told to bring back to the ranch."

"Why? By who? What ranch?" She glances around looking for something—anything—that could serve as a weapon. Propped near the door of the barn, a few yards off, a Garden Weasel, with its metal spurs for tilling new soil to the surface. Charlie can only imagine how it would feel raking it across this guy's face, but even with the reach provided by the long handle it would offer her little range. Inside the barn she knows where Grady keeps a couple rifles and ammo—they had a coyote problem a few seasons back.

"Don't bother, princess," the other voice, female, taunts. "We've got you outnumbered four-to-one—though we'd rather not spill your blood. We need that."

As if on cue, a hand clasps down on either shoulder. Two men have enough time to sneer at her before the headlights of her truck and the loud thunk-thunk of a large animal rolling over the grill of a vehicle catch three of the four intruders off-guard. Charlie sees Grady behind the wheel, grinning as wide as the Cheshire Cat as he mows down one of the men. He starts honking the horn, an almost melodic series of long and short bursts. Morse code: run.

"What the—" one man cries out.

"I thought you tied him up!" the other accuses.

"I did! Old coot musta slipped out somehow!"

As an argument ensues, the truck engine revs. Charlie twists out of their surprise-weakened grasp and bolts for the barn. She slips inside, lodging a stray metal pipe through the handles before taking off to where she knows Grady keeps the rifles. She hears chaos outside, but follows cover as best she can anyway in case she is being followed.

She climbs the retractable ladder to the hayloft, winding the crank to reel it up and out of arm's reach of anyone who may have followed her. He keeps the rifles here because the large windows afford him the best view of his pastures—and property. This barn, the farmhouse, the shed, each grain silo—all the buildings were designed and built by him, each with their own quirks like retractable ladders and tunnels running between buildings underneath the property and, rumor has it, a doomsday bunker that Grady won't admit to and that Charlie, despite hours of dedicated childhood exploration, could never find.

The Morse code was something he insisted she learn one summer and she obliged, being eight and thinking the made-up spy and end-of-the-world scenarios fun. Even a couple years ago, when she found herself sent to her room with the anger and angst caused by parents who just didn't understand, she'd tap out cuss words on her walls so her defiance could go unpunished. She would smile at the memory if it could break through the panic.

She finds the rifles loaded, ready, and with enough ammunition to prove the doomsday bunker theory at the very least plausible. She positions herself at a window, off to the side, the barrel just at the sill. With the scope, a luxury she is unaccustomed to, she can see everything happening down below unfold like a movie. Charlie learned to shoot before she learned to ride a bike, on an old rifle with iron sights that was too heavy for her. The recoil knocked her on her butt but she never missed a target.

She takes a deep breath and squeezes the trigger.

Little do they know, her dad's called her Annie Oakley ever since she took down all seven glass Coke bottles in only seven shots with her six-year-old butt planted firmly in the dirt.

24

Now

LELAND WAITS OUTSIDE THE DOOR TO THE COUNCIL chambers as we arrive and guides me inside without a word to either me or Caius. He wears the same plastered-on smile as before, betraying no sign of what verdict the Council may have reached.

"The girl is armed," Brantley announces as we enter, squinting at me. He leans back in his chair, smirking.

Leland waves him off with an uninterested sigh. "A breach of etiquette, not a crime. Besides," he continues, "who in this room isn't either armed or themselves a weapon?" A sound like a chuckle snakes amongst the Elders assembled, the first time I've seen them remotely collegial on the whole. I am not put at ease. Hyenas' strength is in their numbers, after all, and too many hungry eyes fall to the pendant on my chest.

Though they bid me to sit, I do not. I stand behind the empty chair, spine straight, arms crossed, jaw set in a hard line. Our hearts do not beat, but it's amazing what sensations the body remembers in times like these. For a moment I swear I can hear the ocean of my blood coursing through my veins. I struggle to keep my Beast dormant. To show the Beast is to show fear and to show fear is to show weakness.

In the Everlasting, as in mortals—as in every living thing—there are two reactions to fear: fight and flight. Sometimes flight means survival, means recognizing one stands outnumbered or outgunned. Sometimes flight means biding one's time. This is not cowardly.

Sometimes to survive one must fight. As I

silently measure how many steps I took from the door to where I stand, the revolver at my thigh presses into my skin. I am flanked by six Elders who've survived centuries, perhaps thousands of years, some relying on flight and some personifying massacre. How much blood could I spill before one of them took me down? To fight here means to die here. Not survival, but also not cowardice.

Temperance's honeyed words startle me from thought. "Delilah, darling—please sit."

"I will stand, thank you." Though met with a shrug, my response rouses her Beast, a subtle shift in her energy that I can feel: a Gift of my Blood and, knowing her relationship with Zeke, not one she could remain oblivious to.

"She certainly is her Usher's Childe, is she not?" Alistair sneers.

Caught off-guard by the combative tone, I growl.

That's the thing about the Everlasting: they often mirror themselves. What they can inspire in others, others with the right Gifts could manipulate in them. Temperance can calm the Beast where others can only hope to get out of its way; the price being a tax on her own. Where I can sense the ebb and flow of the Beast in others, I wear my emotions close to the surface if I don't spend considerable effort to bury them. And that, of course, demands a price.

Of all the Gifts I inherited from Zeke, this I took to an extreme.

"Oh hush, child . . . " Though Temperance's tone mocks, my Beast retreats to a quiet inner corner. An overt show of dominance, not even pretending to soothe me with a reasonable address but with an insult.

"Can we just get to the verdict?" I ask through a clenched jaw.

"Verdict?" Leland chuckles, shaking his head. "You misunderstand the situation, Delilah. The Council has summoned you to thank you for your insight into the murder of Ezekiel Winter and put your mind at ease regarding what steps will be taken next."

A glance between the faces of the assembled Elders makes it difficult to believe I am here to be commended for anything, so I speak. "You said 'murder' . . ."

"Indeed we did," Leland starts. "The Council convened after meeting with you. We discussed your vision, as well as how it might be relevant to the current state of affairs between the Keepers and the Praedari."

"You speak as though the vote were unanimous . . . " Alistair grumbles. Leland shoots him a look before returning his attention to me. "The Council deems it best for sect security to treat Zeke's murder as a declaration of war."

"Delilah, this means that if there's anything else you can tell us—anything else you might remember—"

I don't hear more of what Evelyn has to say, instead catching Temperance in my peripheral vision. Did Zeke confide in her? If he did, has she already told the Council about what I saw the night of my Becoming? If she hasn't, why not? What will happen if she has and I do not?

"There's more," I announce. A hushed whisper breaks out amongst the Council members, my voice startling even myself.

୨୧

"There's more," my voice, not under my command, states before launching into the vision I had at my Becoming. Sometimes sharing a vision causes me to lapse into a fugue-like state. Under these conditions, my retelling captures the most details. Sometimes I can only remember bits and pieces, always jumbled and often cryptic. This time, though, it's as if the vision is pulled from me.

A low ringing in my ear when I finish. Six seated figures stare at me, a collection of pursed lips and furrowed brows. If Temperance is shaken or surprised by my offering up the rest of my vision to the Council, she does not show it, instead mimicking their judgment. Silence, except the ringing.

A figure stands. Taller than I would have guessed or taller now than the night before, I'm not sure. His gray robes shift around him, almost as though they live and do as he bids. Just as last time I hadn't noticed him until he desired it, only vaguely aware that a sixth person sat in a sixth chair just as they had the last time I visited these chambers. Even in recollection his presence remains inexplicably obfuscated.

Moments melt into his robes, becoming the fiber of which they're woven. I wonder if the others can see this or if it is a flash of insight, a sort of partial vision while I'm conscious and aware. His unflinching gaze causes the hairs on the back of my neck to rise.

"Delilah, daughter of Ezekiel Winter, granddaughter of Ismae the Bloody . . . " A voice bellows in my mind using the old parlance, the word from before the Keeper's adopted *Childe*—meaning one of noble birth—to denote the relationship between Usher and the one they Ushered. Before the Keepers and Praedari came into being, Zeke would tell me, the Everlasting didn't need to rely on language to elevate their standing. A quick scan of the other Elders assembled leads me to believe I am not alone in hearing the voice. "By decree of this Council you must find the mortals from your vision and—"

"The Council never voted on the girl's direct involvement—" Brantley interjects.

Enoch's head turns towards the interruption, the deliberate movement cutting off the rest of the chameleon's argument. The Eldest whispers something unintelligible in his direction, the pupils of his eyes changing to milk-white for just a moment.

Brantley starts making gagging and sputtering sounds, his hands clutching his throat in the universal sign indicating *choking* as we look on in horror. His tongue elongates and writhes for what feels to us like minutes, to Brantley, I can only imagine, longer—then erupts into thousands of maggots. What would be howls of pain become gurgles as blood and maggots build a gory blockade in his long-dead airway. The pain too much to bear, he falls to the floor, limp. His eyes do not close. No one dares move to help him.

Enoch returns his attention to me. Every muscle in my body tensed, ready to spring. I feel my pupils dilate, my Beast nudging me to make the age-old decision: fight or flight. Then a hand on my own. Temperance. At her touch my Beast reluctantly quiets. I cast a grateful glance her way, her meddling for once welcome. She gives a slight nod of acknowledgement.

This time Enoch speaks, his voice gravel and silk and ocean at once.

"This is your chance to avenge your beloved, Delilah."

Dizzy, I can't help but glance at poor Brantley.

Enoch speaks as though I have a choice but I can't shake the feeling that there is only one right answer.

"Brantley will heal, with time, as the Everlasting do. What I'm offering you is a way to heal *now*."

"A decree isn't an offer . . . " The words spew ahead of rational thought. If long pauses and awkward silences could build an empire, the Council has put the Roman Empire to shame sixty times over this night. I swear I can feel tiny pinpoints of wriggling inside my tongue as I anticipate my punishment.

"Indeed, it is not. Choice is often an illusion."

"Why should I find the kids rather than seek out Zeke's murderer? How would this avenge my Usher?"

Enoch considers me a moment, the corners of his mouth turning just slightly downward. "As Keepers, our job is protect the mortal world—both from knowledge of our kind and from the Praedari who would openly hunt them. If it is indeed the Praedari who've killed your Usher, your quest to find the children should lead you right to their hive. If your vision is correct, I can only imagine the horrors that await them—and humanity—should they not be found."

"Why me?" I ask, not quite convinced.

"The rage of Ismae the Bloody still sings in your veins, Delilah. Will you avenge your Usher and beloved by protecting the mortals from your vision, or will Ezekiel's sacrifice have been in vain? Will you honor your Blood or deny your legacy? A decision of this gravity cannot hope to be encountered twice by even the Eldest Everlasting. It is a blessing, but it does not come without risk. It is a chance for glory, as well as closure. You may take some time to decide."

"That is not necessary," I declare, stepping forward. "I've made my decision."

Now

TEMPERANCE ESCORTS ME FROM THE COUNCIL chambers this time. She waits to speak until we are out of earshot of the other Elders. Caius lingers by the stairs, making very little effort to conceal his eavesdropping.

"Delilah, I know we had a moment in there but I really hope you come, in time, to see me as an ally." Her words meet silence, so she continues. "As Leland said, you have the full support of the Council in your mission. Whatever resources you may need—"

I hold a hand up to stop her.

"You're going to say 'I don't need your help,' aren't you?" Temperance says.

"Close. I was going to go with 'I don't need a babysitter. Or six,'" I retort.

She sighs, rubbing her furrowed brow. "None of us have lived as long as we have without having to rely on someone once in a while. Usually it's our Ushers, until we've outlived them. You're like us now, Delilah. With Zeke gone you must make your own way, but you can't do it alone. You can dive deep for what you're seeking like he did, but eventually you must surface for air."

"And what do you know about what I'm going through? I'm *nothing* like you," I challenge.

"I know that the decision you made didn't seem like it had multiple choices—but it did. That you could only fathom one shows your dedication to his memory."

Caius takes a few steps towards us. "Let it rest, Siren. Can't you see she's been through enough?"

"I'm surprised you'd care, Conqueror. Or that she'd let you rush to her defense."

"She's my ward."

"Not as of now. On behalf of the Council I am awarding her Autonomy, since her Usher didn't have the chance to petition for it himself. She is ready. It is what Ezekiel would have wanted," she adds softly for my benefit.

Caius snorts. "Autonomy? That's a strong word for such a short leash."

Temperance rolls her eyes. "Is this going to be another oppressor versus the oppressed diatribe? Because I must warn you sunrise isn't far off. You'd have to make it quick. Wouldn't want to see you burn, Conqueror. Haven't you had enough of the smell of burning flesh?"

"Independence must be taken by force and protected, not given," he argues.

"She's right, Caius," I say, hoping to diffuse the tension I'm exhausted of. "We should settle in for the day."

He shrugs, putting his hand up in front of him as in resignation and heading up the staircase.

"Delilah," Temperance reaches out to touch my shoulder, "I *am* in your corner. I want you to take this." She draws a small, navy blue velvet box from somewhere I can't see. "Don't open it until you're far away from here."

I glance up the stairs but Caius is already outside. I nod and tuck the box into my jacket before following him.

Now

"SO WHAT'S THIS KID'S NAME?" A FEMALE VOICE asks as Hunter comes to.

"How should I know?" a male responds.

"Do you two ever listen to briefings?" a familiarly-accented voice sighs.

"I missed the memo."

"Hunter. His name is Hunter."

"That's ironic," the female snorts before belting out a few bars of Alanis Morissette.

Hunter is lying on his side in the fetal position, scratchy fabric like a welcome mat that smells vaguely of gasoline and soil against his face. He sees darkness despite his eyes being open, the slight pressure of cloth against his eyelashes as he blinks. The hum of tires on freeway and the familiar lurch of being in a vehicle. A window is open, just a crack by the sound, the cool air a respite from the stuffiness at least. He's bound at the wrists with his arms behind his back with some sort of thin plastic; at the ankles with something he can't quite feel through his jeans.

He nods his head against the carpeting, trying to slide the blindfold down so he can see but it holds tight. Now his face itches. He stretches his legs out straight trying to get a sense of how much space he's confined to, taking care to make as little noise as possible.

"Who sings that song?" the accented-man asks.

"Alanis Mor—"

"Yeah, let's keep it that way," he interrupts, his pleased smile evident in his voice.

The hollow thump of someone smacking

someone in the chest, hard, and then the vehicle swerves a moment. Hunter winces and shrinks back to fetal.

"Shut it, Pierce."

A phone rings.

"It's Victor," Pierce announces. The squabbling falls silent.

"Hey boss. Target acquired. Of course it wasn't too much trouble—we're professionals. No, he's fine, not a hair harmed on his little mortal head, just as you instructed. As you Americans are fond of saying, this hasn't been our first rodeo. Straight to the ranch, got it."

"'This hasn't been our first rodeo'?" The girl teases. "God you're lame talking to the higher-ups. Don't you have rodeos in the UK?"

"Shut up, Lydia—"

Someone turns the radio up. A broadcast about an explosion in a downtown metro station is met with hoots and hollers from up front. Someone high-fives someone else.

"We made the news!" Lydia cheers. "Sorry I doubted you, Johnny—credit where it's due."

"Tagging at the scene of the explosion links the incident to a string of violent petty crimes and vandalisms that have taken place throughout the city," the voice on the radio reports.

Hunter repeats their names in his head. Pierce. Lydia. Johnny. *The metro explosion, why I'm here.*

"Huh? Guess we weren't the only Praedari in town . . ."

"That was us," a rather sluggish voice offers.

"No, the metro explosion was us—the rest of this crime wave must've been someone else . . ."

"Quiet," someone shushes.

The newscast continues, "Spray painted in red in the tunnel at Spring Street Station—"

The three voices from up front join the broadcaster in a bright chorus. "It is not the burden of the lion to protect the gazelle."